D1497932

SOME CLOUDS

SOME CLOUDS

Paco Ignacio Taibo II

Translated by William I. Neuman

Viking

VIKING
Published by the Penguin Group
Viking Penguin, a division of Penguin Books USA Inc.,
375 Hudson Street, New York, New York 10014, U.S.A.
Penguin Books Ltd, 27 Wrights Lane,
London W8 5TZ, England
Penguin Books Australia Ltd, Ringwood,
Victoria, Australia
Penguin Books Canada Ltd, 10 Alcorn Avenue, Suite 300,
Toronto, Ontario, Canada M4V 3B2
Penguin Books (N.Z.) Ltd, 182–190 Wairau Road,
Auckland 10, New Zealand

Penguin Books Ltd, Registered Offices:
Harmondsworth, Middlesex, England

First published in 1992 by Viking Penguin,
a division of Penguin Books USA Inc.

1 3 5 7 9 10 8 6 4 2
Translation copyright © Paco Ignacio Taibo II and
William I. Neuman, 1992
All rights reserved

Originally published in Mexico as *Algunas Nubes* by Leega Literaria, 1985.
© Paco Ignacio Taibo II. © Editora y Distribuidora Leega, S. A. de C. V.
Mexico, D. F.

Library of Congress Cataloging in Publication Data
Taibo, Paco Ignacio, 1949–
[Algunas nubes. English]
Some clouds / by Paco Ignacio Taibo II ; translated by William I. Neuman.
p.   cm.
Translation of: Algunas nubes.
ISBN 0-670-83825-X
I. Title.
PQ7298.3.A58A7813   1992
863—dc20   91-44629

Printed in the United States of America
Set in Times Roman
Designed by Virginia Norey

This novel is for my friend Liliana, who's probably wandering around somewhere near Córdoba, for my friend Jorge Castañeda, somewhere in the south of *el DF*, and for Héctor Rodríguez, somewhere in the cave on Tabasco Street.

"The rose of syphilis bloomed by night and by day."
—*Michael Gold*

"Nothing is as it seems."
—*Justin Playfair to Mildred Watson*

SOME CLOUDS

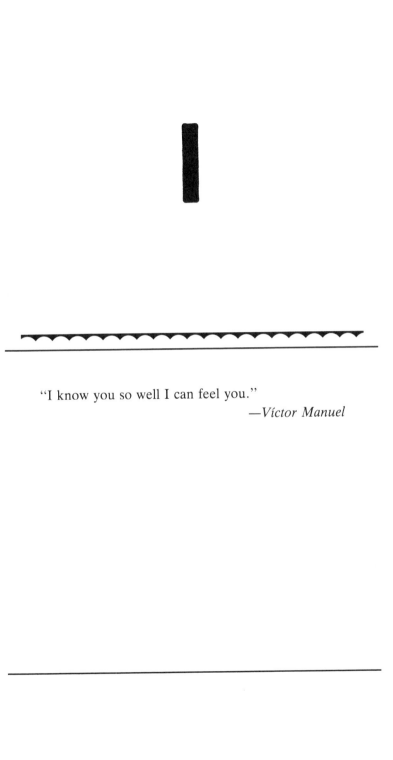

I

"I know you so well I can feel you."
—*Víctor Manuel*

He was sitting in the last chair under the last lonely palm tree, drinking beer out of a bottle and cleaning the sand off a pile of small shells. The sugary chords of a bolero drifted over from a palm-thatched hut where a man in a lime green shirt washed glasses in a bucket of water.

It was her all right. He could see her coming, guessed it was her rounding the curve in the highway and dropping down along the upper part of the beach where the construction company trucks had packed the sand down hard. He saw her coming, hid his head behind the pile of shells, and downed the rest of his beer. He didn't have anything against his sister in particular; normally they got along just fine. But he could feel it inside him: with Elisa came changes he wasn't ready for.

He was tired, beat, blown out, flat, limp, weary, wasted, in love with a bottle of beer and a bolero and the soft murmur of the waves. Full of a deep yearning for this lonely palm tree, the afternoon sun, those few fat jolly clouds dotting the sky. But, while he could hide his eyes, he couldn't keep his ears from hearing the sound of her motorcycle drawing closer along the beach, and he had to accept the idea that the vacation he'd been taking from himself was coming to an end.

He looked up from the pile of shells and smiled at her with his one good eye. Elisa cut the engine and coasted the last few yards along the sand. Her helmet was strapped behind her on top of a small knapsack, and she wore a long red scarf around her neck. That was so much like Elisa: the scarf, her hair trailing behind her in the breeze, the bike rolling along the beach.

"Just as I thought," she said, "lazing around under the last palm tree on the beach."

"Check out those clouds over there," he said, just to have something to say.

"I wish there were more of them. I've been totally frying myself for the last fifty miles," Elisa said, striding over to put herself rudely, indelicately, between her brother's arms.

Hector hugged her fiercely. Maybe she was bringing something besides the heat of the road, her sweaty shirt, the harsh sun in the blue Sinaloa sky, but she was his sister after all.

" 'Nother coupla beers, engineer?" asked the man

tending the little bar. He watched them with a broad grin.

"Make it four, Marcial," said Hector through Elisa's hair, surprised to discover it didn't smell like that lemon shampoo their mother had always used on them, that smell that came back to him now and then like so many other smells from his childhood.

Elisa stepped back, brushing the hair from her face, and dropped into a chair.

"This is the most beautiful place in the world," she said.

"No. It's the second most beautiful place in the world," answered Hector, sitting down. The metal chair sank another inch into the sand.

"Right, the most beautiful place in the world hasn't been discovered yet. Isn't that how it goes?"

"No. The most beautiful place in the world is about half an hour from here, down the beach, that-a-way," said Hector, pointing.

"That's hard to believe," she said. She stared out at the ocean, trying to tune into her brother's rhythm, get in touch with the peacefulness of the place. No easy thing, coming off a full day on the road at eighty miles an hour, the thoughts buzzing around inside her head at twice that speed.

The barman, whom everyone called La Estrellita and who'd inherited the restaurant from his uncle, came out from behind the wooden counter, walked across the sand, and set the four bottles tinkling against each other onto the table. The late afternoon heat played off the frosted bottles while the ocean purred on, the light starting to change. The same two fat clouds hung motionless, nailed against the sky.

"So what's new, Hector? What have you been doing with yourself?" asked Elisa.

"There's not much to tell. I've been working for a fisherman's co-op out of Puerto Guayaba, about a mile up the coast, helping them build a sewer system for the town. But it's been a long time, I've had to study about as much as I've had to work. I forgot a lot of stuff. Engineering stuff, flow rates, specs, that kind of thing. So I work some, take long walks along the beach. I'm the Lone Engineer. Sort of like the Lone Ranger, but without the gun. . . . That's about all there is to it. It's somewhere in between being an engineer in a factory and being a detective. But a lot lonelier than either one of them. . . . You don't kill anybody, you don't rip anybody off. You work with real people, they say hello to you in the morning, you hang around and shoot the shit together. You don't owe anybody anything. I like it that way."

Hector looked at his sister with his one good eye. The other lay unmoving in its scarred socket, like a decoration, staring at nothing or looking fixedly out at the waves, the hovering gulls.

"You quit wearing your eyepatch?" asked Elisa.

Hector lifted his hand to his face and touched his glass eye, running his fingers along the scar.

"It's a pain in the butt. The sand gets under it and then it gets all teary. . . . It's like something out of a horror story. . . . Some old lady who puts her dentures in a glass of water by her bed and then in the middle of the night they come alive and bite her in the neck."

"That's gross, Hector."

"How about you? How's Carlos? How'd you . . . uh . . . how'd you find me?"

"Your landlord, The Wiz, back in Mexico City, he told me where you were. He said you asked him to send you some books every now and then. I thought about it for a week or so and then the day before yesterday I jumped on my bike, and here I am. It wasn't too hard to find you."

"No, I just thought . . ."

They looked at each other. Elisa reached across, took her brother's hand, and squeezed it. But she let go quickly, not sure she was sending the right message, picked up a bottle of beer, and touched it to Hector's.

Six months, one week, and two days ago, Hector had killed a man. That didn't matter too much. Another man's life was another man's life. The guy deserved to die. The problem was that in the middle of the gunfight a stray bullet had found the head of an eight-year-old boy. The boy didn't die, but he was going to be a vegetable for the rest of his life. Hector didn't think the bullet was his. It was the other guy's, it had to be. No one had connected Hector with the gunfight. The dead man took his name and his credit cards with him to the grave. No one else knew anything about it. Except Hector, who couldn't forget.

He went to the hospital once to see the kid. He found the room, the boy covered in bandages, his empty stare. That same night he left the city, without knowing where he was going, not that night, or the next one, or the next. The story's simple enough. When a man can't get away from himself, he does what he can to get away from everything else, he leaves home, leaves town, leaves the country. It's all a matter of running fast enough and far enough until he loses his own shadow. And now here was Elisa, come to remind him of everything again . . . the kid in the oxygen tent, his empty eyes.

"So what's up, Sis? You come to take care of me, or did you come to take me away from my little spiritual retreat here? What're you afraid of? Maybe you should have just stopped back there at the last beach up the road and gone for a swim. Left me in peace."

Elisa looked at her brother, and her eyes went hard. The music burst out again from the *palapa,* the same bolero by Manzanero that Hector had been listening to over the last few months.

"Give me a break, Hector. If there's anything I can't stand it's self-pity. I can smell it from a mile off. You know me, I'm a goddamn expert in it. Or did you forget already? I spend half the time fucking up and the other half wishing I hadn't, feeling guilty and sorry for myself, and then starting the whole damn process over again. I'm your sister, Hector. Remember me? Now I wish I'd never come."

"It's okay, Elisa. Feeling sorry for ourselves is a family tradition," said Hector. He took hold of her hand without looking at her.

"It'd be nice to spend a few days hanging out on the beach. I brought some books. I brought a picture of this boyfriend I had back in grade school who I haven't seen in I don't know how long. I brought a couple of Roy Brown tapes. You know Roy Brown? The Puerto Rican Bob Dylan. I even brought a book to learn how to play the flute. . . . I can't believe it! I forgot the fucking flute. I'm not in any hurry, Hector. There's no rush. I've got a whole week to decide if I'm going to tell you what I came here to tell you. Maybe I won't even tell you anything at all. What do you think?"

Hector stared up at the palm tree. Thirty yards above their heads palm fronds tossed in a light breeze.

"Books?" he said. "What'd you bring? I've already read all three volumes of Runciman's *History of the Crusades* four times over. That goddamn Merlin hasn't sent me one mystery novel since I left. And of course, there's no bookstore around here. You can't even get a newspaper."

He didn't wait for Elisa's answer, but tried instead to put on his carefree beach-bum look, tried to think about something else. But Elisa wasn't that easily fooled.

The routines of his life in the little town weren't enough to keep his mind from whatever it was Elisa had come to tell him. Sometimes he was convinced everything had been decided from the moment he saw her driving her bike down onto the beach. All he could do was wait, take the time to readjust, accept the inevitable: his return to the city. Sometimes he pretended he'd be able to ignore the call of the wild and stay where he was, a kind of White Fang tamed by solitude. He went back and forth. One day deciding that destiny didn't exist, the next day convincing himself that it did; and so it went, while he waited for Elisa to make up her mind.

It turned out Elisa was as crazy about his Aznavour

records as he was, and they spent whole afternoons together listening to the singer's honey-sweet romantic bal-
lads, watching the grass grow, watching a lilac bush.
Hector went for walks around town, drank beer, they
sat around together and reminisced about a family trip
to Acapulco when they were kids. And all the time he
kept going back to look at himself in the bathroom
mirror.

The most definite sign came when he left off drinking
beer and went back to Pepsis and lemon crush. This new
sobriety was directly connected to the seriousness of his
impending return. Beer was one of the luxuries of loneliness. Finally on Friday, with four more days still to go
in Elisa's week, he tried to give himself up.

"Come on, Sis, out with it. What'd you come to tell
me?" he asked, sitting down on the floor in front of her.
She sat on the couch, reading a book of poems by Luis
Rogelio Nogueras.

Elisa looked up from the book and smiled.

"You've still got four more days, what's your hurry?"

"Give me a break, Elisa. I didn't have a chance from
the start. As soon as you told me you were going to wait
a week, that was it. I'd already lost."

"I just don't want to feel guilty about it. I'm trying to
be a good girl. I don't want to pressure you into
anything."

"To each his own, Elisa. It's my fault for coming here
to hide away in the first place, and it's your fault for
coming here to take me back again."

"There are still four days left, Hector. Don't worry
about it. You're just curious, that's all."

"What do you mean, don't worry about it? Four days from now I'll probably agree to anything. Now at least I might be able to defend myself against your craziness."

"How about if you give me two more days? You wouldn't want to spoil my vacation, would you?"

"Tomorrow afternoon, Elisa. All right? Tomorrow afternoon. And however it turns out, whether or not I accept whatever it is you've got for me, we stay here another day together."

"It's a deal," said Elisa, and she went back to the poem she'd been reading before.

The meeting took place on the beach. Elisa had gone ahead on her bike and Hector followed on foot. It was late in the day, the sun going down like a picture post-card, the waves beating against the sand with a melodic murmur. Elisa wore a white bikini and when she came out of the water Hector could see the scars from when she'd had her appendix taken out. She was an attractive woman, shining wet skin, her body outlined against the dying sun. He stuck his face in the sand to get away from the idea of incest, but it followed him there. So he took the idea between his hands and dissolved it little by little in the sand, running it through his fingers. A light breeze blew along the beach. It was a travel agent's dream: palm trees, a burning sun sinking into the water, a subtle wind to break the heat of the fading day. Everything just like it was supposed to be.

Elisa slipped into a yellow terry-cloth dress and kissed

her brother on top of his head. Hector looked up at her and smiled.

Hector Belascoarán Shayne had two exotic last names, a degree in engineering from the National University, and one eye less than most people. He was thirty-five years old, with an ex-wife, an ex-lover, one brother, one sister, a denim suit that made him look more like a social anthropologist than a detective, a .38 automatic in a drawer in his office in Mexico City, a slight limp from an old bullet wound in his right leg, and a private investigator's licence he'd gotten through a correspondence course. He had a marked predilection for soft drinks, lemon-scented aftershave, crab salad, the bossa nova, and certain Hemingway novels (the first ones and the next to the next to the last). His heroes were Justin Playfair, Michel Strogoff, John Reed, Buenaventura Durruti, Capablanca, and Zorro (although he knew he was never going to get very far with a cemetery-full of heroes like that one.) He slept less than six hours a night, he liked the soft sound ideas made when they came together inside his head, and he'd spent the last five years bearing up under the strange weight of an inexplicable fatigue, awash in a sea of memories, reliving wasted passions, idiot love affairs, old routines that had once seemed exciting. He didn't think too highly of himself in general, although he did have a good deal of respect for his capacity for bullheaded stubbornness.

Maybe all of this somehow explains—aside from the fact that explanations tend to be unnecessary—why Hector kept playing with the sand until he'd dug himself a regular-sized hole in which he buried the dead man, dead six months now, and the injured boy.

Elisa waited until the sand was smooth again and then led Hector back toward the house, preparing herself for the story she had to tell, working hard to resist the drowsy, gentle murmur of the waves.

"There's no such thing as innocent wealth."
—*Eduardo Galeano*

"It's not my story, so I'm going to tell it to you just like I heard it. Once there were three brothers," said Elisa. "One went to high school with me and married Ana—my friend Anita. Little Orphan Annie. Remember?"

Hector nodded. Anita, a perky little redhead who was popular in high school because she could speak three languages. Elisa would bring her home for lunch every now and then. She was good at crossword puzzles and would sit down to lend a hand to Old Man Belascoarán, to the rest of the family's amazement. Ana, who used to stay up nights at boarding school reading the dictionary. Hector could see her with her green book bag, full of wonderful strange things, heavier than a bagful of bricks. Little redheaded Anita, fascinated by the Chinese novels of Malraux. (When Hector read Malraux many years later he remembered how he'd pigheadedly turned down Ana's offer to loan him the books, and he'd kicked himself over another lost opportunity.) All right, so, Anita. What about her?

"So Anita got married to this guy and they went off to the U.S. to go to medical school. The other two brothers stayed home and spent their time throwing away their old man's money. One day Anita's husband got a phone call and rushed back to Mexico City. His father had died. A heart attack. Nothing unusual. But that's where things started to get complicated. On the day of the father's funeral, while Anita's husband was still on his way to Mexico, they found the other two brothers in the old family house. One of them was shot to death, and the other one, the youngest one, they found him sitting in front of his dead brother like a vegetable, totally out of his mind. He couldn't talk, it was like he'd forgotten how, they couldn't get him to say a word. Now he's living in a nuthouse in . . . where is it . . . Cuernavaca, I think, just the same as he was the day they found him. Doesn't say a damn thing. What do you think about that?"

"Is that it?"

"That's just the beginning," said Elisa, hoping that Hector would take the bait: three brothers, one a doctor married to redheaded Anita, one of them shot to death, and the other one out of his mind, sitting in front of his murdered sibling.

"What happened next?"

They were sitting on the porch of the little house two

hundred yards from the ocean. Hector had brought out a bottle of Pepsi. Elisa had brought along two more, as if to say that the story was going to be a long one, demanding all of her brother's deductive abilities, stimulated by the Pepsi-Colas. Hector, who didn't believe in logical thinking, hadn't even brought a notebook. He just sat and listened. Waiting for something. Waiting to know where to start, a street, a corner. Something to lead him into other people's lives, other people's deaths, other people's ghosts. One way or another it all boiled down to a question of streets, avenues, parks, it was a question of walking, of pecking around and sorting out. Hector only knew one method. He'd throw himself bodily into someone else's story until the story became his own. He tried to picture the streets around the insane asylum in Cuernavaca. He didn't like the idea.

"Later on, Anita and her husband went to see the younger brother, they talked to the doctors. Nothing. The kid never said a word. He'd gone away and he wasn't coming back. At least that's what the doctors said. The cops said it was a burglary, they said there'd been a rash of them lately and that the other brother probably tried to resist and got himself shot. They figured the nutty brother saw the whole thing, but as long as he couldn't talk there wasn't anything they could do about it. That's as far as it went where the police were concerned."

Hector decided not to ask any more questions. Elisa was going to tell the story in her own way and it was better not to interrupt her.

"Anita and her husband went back to the U.S."

"Where?" asked Hector, breaking his promise to himself.

"Where what? Where'd they go?"

"Yeah."

"New York. They worked together in the kidney ward at the hospital at some university."

"Hmm," said Hector. New York sounded a hell of a lot better than Cuernavaca.

"They'd been back in New York a week when the papers arrived from the lawyer, along with the bank statements and the rest of the stuff about the inheritance. That's when they got the big surprise. The old man, Anita's father-in-law, had owned a few furniture stores in downtown Mexico City. Three of them, I guess. Anita's husband figured he had some money coming his way, because there'd always been enough in the family, more than enough really, plus a little extra for vacations, cars for the kids, private universities, that kind of thing. But he had no idea how things really stood. It turned out the old guy had over one hundred and sixty million pesos in stocks, nearly twenty million in his checking account, fifty-six million in an account in another bank, and I don't know how much more in real estate. He had a house in Guadalajara, another one in Guaymas, he owned a bottling plant in Puebla. The old guy was rolling in dough. It was incredible. Everywhere they looked there was something else. He owned shares in a bunch of companies that they'd never even heard of. There were safe deposit boxes in a bunch of different banks, boats in Mazatlán, clothing stores in Monterrey. And it was all spread out across the country. Anita's husband went back to Mexico City to take charge of the estate, have his brother declared legally insane, and find out what was in the safe deposit boxes. Ten days later he went back to New York. That night somebody stabbed him to death in the lobby of their apartment building. In just two months the whole family was wiped out, the dad, the three brothers, all of them. Anita was scared to death."

Hector remembered how Elisa and Anita used to lock themselves in Elisa's bedroom, smoke cigarettes, play the guitar, and sing Joan Baez songs. He'd complain that he couldn't get any studying done, but they always ignored him. He tried to remember which one played the guitar.

"Which one of you played the guitar?" he asked.

Elisa looked at him for a few long seconds. Hector smiled at the absurdity of his question.

"Me. Anita was a better singer, but she didn't know how to play the guitar. How'd you remember?"

"I must have been a real jerk back then. Instead of hanging out with you guys and singing Joan Baez songs I spent all my time reading bullshit books about soil science."

"Whadaya know. I thought you'd never admit it."

"So what did Anita do then?"

"First she tried to find the rest of the family, but there wasn't any. She was the only one left. There weren't even any distant relatives. All that was left was their big old house in Polanco, complete with bloodstains on the rug, and the bedroom where the old man had died in his sleep. She shut herself up in the house and tried to pretend nothing had happened, that all she had to do was wait around for someone to come and wake her up from her nightmare, take her out to a double feature of cowboy movies, and buy her a box of popcorn and everything would be okay again."

"And?"

"Finally, one day the family lawyer showed up and told her she was a millionaire, and I mean *millionaire*. He said he'd help her clear up the whole mess with the inheritance. Anita went and checked into a hotel in the Colonia Roma. I guess she felt really lonely, because she started going through the phone book and calling around trying to find her old friends from ten years ago. That's how she found me."

A hotel in the Colonia Roma in downtown Mexico City. That was something Hector could relate to. It was a lot better than Cuernavaca or New York.

"Where'd she find you?"

"I was over at Mama and Papa's old house one day to pay the caretaker and pick up a couple of books. I just happened to be there when she called."

"So what's Anita want from me?"

"Hold on, I'm not finished yet," Elisa said. She got up and went into the bathroom. Hector polished off his first bottle of Pepsi with a long swallow, took out a cigarette, knocked it on the table a few times, and lit up. The Delicado straights he'd been smoking lately were full of little sticks and branches. He had to shake the garbage out before he could smoke them. Hector looked at the cigarette in his hand with distrust, waiting to see if it burned like a peace pipe or simply refused to draw at all. An idea crossed his mind.

"Elisa. . . . Did they kill Anita?"

"Almost." Her voice came indistinctly from the other side of the bathroom door.

Shit. That was too much, too complicated. Just complicated enough for the story to start to draw him in, hypnotize him. But he didn't want Anita dead. To get himself going he needed to feel something, some kind of sympathy, and he needed someone alive to feel it for. He was sick and tired of so many corpses. He'd had his fill of love for the dead.

Elisa came out of the bathroom, drying her hands on her scarf.

"Almost, they almost killed her, but that comes later. She called me up and we got together and had lunch. We had a lot of fun. The poor girl was in shock, she was like a sleepwalker. Then one day she called and said she'd been to talk with the lawyer and that she wanted to see me. I went to her hotel and she told me what had happened. The lawyer showed up all nervous and sweating and told her she'd be able to keep a few million but if she wanted the rest of the old man's money she'd have to go talk to a Mr. Melgar, Mr. Arturo Melgar. The next day they came after her. . . ."

"The Rat," said Hector.

"One and the same." Elisa nodded. "Your old college buddy."

"Shit," was all Hector said. He let the cigarette go out between his fingers.

"Too many things happen in the foreground, and we don't know anything about what happens in the background."

—*Heinrich Böll*

Elisa left the next morning and Hector felt her absence in the house. It wasn't her warmth he missed so much. The weather was hot enough to make up for that. It had more to do with certain vibrations in the air, a lack of peace. The days had been sweet and slow in the week Elisa was there. Now he felt the rush again, the city insinuating itself into the tropical air, the inevitability of his return slipping in through the open windows while he chewed his eggs and bacon on the porch, staring out at the sea.

"I'm going to miss all of this," he told himself. *This* was the sea. He didn't want to waste a lot of time in good-byes, so he packed his suitcase in less than half an hour, filled three cardboard boxes with things he didn't care if he lost on the bus trip home, and walked into town to say so long to his friends at work, the old woman at the corner store, and the guy who ran the movie theater (one show per week plus a Sunday matinee for the kids). He didn't bother going down to the dock; none of his buddies would be around at that time of day anyway. He skipped city hall and only went over to the construction company office to pick up his last check and let them know he was going away. The secretary tried to get him to wait until the boss arrived, so he told her that his grandfather had just died and left him an inheritance.

He returned the keys to the car the co-op had let him use sometimes and, without looking back, he said good-bye to the sea.

Hector could go for hours without thinking, feeling no need to string one coherent thought after another. He'd let his mind run on on its own, rambling, connecting stray images, visions, birds, butterflies, memories, daydreams. Now he tuned into the fog channel and didn't tune out again until, sixteen hours after saying good-bye to the last lonely palm tree in Puerto Guayaba, he stepped out of the elevator and stood in front of his office door in Mexico City.

A fat man in an ill-fitting suit stood in front of the frosted glass painted with the familiar names: Belascoarán Shayne—Detective. Gilberto Gómez Letras—Plumber. Carlos Vargas—Upholsterer. Gallo Villarreal—Sewer and Drainage Expert. Hector vaguely remembered seeing the man somewhere before.

"It's about time," said the fat man. "When do they open up around here anyway?"

"Nobody home?" asked Hector innocently.

"Nobody answered when I knocked."

Hector took out his keys and unlocked the door. He was met by a comforting wave of disorder. A half-stripped lilac armchair sat on top of his desk where Carlos Vargas had presumably been working on it. Everything was reassuringly familiar. He smiled at the wall with the pictures of Zapata and Fernando Valenzuela, the newspaper clippings, the girlie pictures from the afternoon papers.

Someone had drawn a hopscotch game in chalk on the wooden floor. Probably El Gallo, in one of his fits of lyricism.

"Make yourself at home," said Hector to the fat man. "You looking for the upholsterer or the plumber?"

"I'm looking for the goddamn detective. You think I'd stand around and wait all this time for a friggin' plumber?"

"*¡Jefe, jefecito santo!* It hasn't been the same around here without you," shouted Carlos Vargas from the doorway, and without wasting time he rushed over to grab Hector's hand in a firm and solemn grip. "It's been boring as hell since you went away. No braless dancing girls, no knifed old ladies with their guts hanging out."

"I guess the detective's me," Hector said to the fat man as he gave the upholsterer a big hug.

"My wife's a no-good whore," said the fat man in the rumpled suit, shooing a fly off Hector's desk with a hand the size of a baseball glove. He looked at Hector blandly.

"Excuse me?" asked the detective. He realized where

he'd seen the fat man before. He was Don Gaspar, the owner of a sandwich shop halfway down the block.

"She's been whoring around on me. She goes out and spends all the dough I give her on black and red panties and frilly bras and stuff, but she never uses 'em with me."

"Maybe she's shy," said Carlos the upholsterer, pretending to concentrate on a black leather executive-style swivel chair, its insides spilling out.

"Shy my ass, she's a friggin' whore."

"That's all very well and good, Don Gaspar. But a detective's got to work with facts," said Hector soothingly.

"That's why I came here. I want you to get me the proof and then I want you to beat the shit out of her . . ."

"Let's get one thing straight, Don Gaspar . . ." began Hector.

"I'll pay you for it. I don't care what it costs."

Hector stared. The fat man made like he was going to pull a flask of brandy out of his hip pocket and break into tears.

"Look, Don Gaspar," said Carlos from his corner of the room. "Don't you worry about a thing. We'll take care of everything, and it won't cost you very much either."

Don Gaspar stared at the upholsterer who stood smiling, his mouth half full of upholstery tacks.

"This guy work with you or what?"

"Something like that," said Hector, glaring at Carlos. The smile froze on the upholsterer's face.

"It's a deal, then," said Don Gaspar.

"We'll need twenty thousand up front," said Carlos.

Don Gaspar stuck a thick hand into his pants pocket and pulled out a wad of wrinkled, sweaty bills. He licked his thumb and counted out the money.

"What's your wife's name? And what's your address?" asked Hector.

"Amalia, Amalia the friggin' whore. We live in Colonia Moderna. I'll write the address down for you. I'm in the restaurant all day, see. That's how come she got to be such a friggin' whore."

Don Gaspar scribbled his address down on an old newspaper and stood up. Without saying another word he trudged toward the door, his enormous shoulders sunk under the terrible weight of Amalia the whore. He shut the door gently behind him.

"Now, do you want to tell me what the hell you think you're doing?" said Hector, turning on Carlos. "Just who do you think's going to go figure out if Don Gaspar's wife's been screwing someone behind his back? And who's going to kick the shit out of her once we figure it out? You're always getting me mixed up in this kind of crap. Here I am, I just get back to town, and you've already got me running after some asshole's cheating wife. I've got a job to do, I don't have time to waste hanging around in lingerie departments trying to find out what color underpants this guy's old lady buys."

"Don't worry. Leave it to me. I'll let you know what happens," said Carlos in a businesslike voice. He picked up the twenty wrinkled thousand-peso notes off the desk and counted them out into two separate piles. Then he picked up the piece of newspaper with Don Gaspar's address, aimed another broad grin at the detective, and walked out the door.

Hector didn't really mind. He was as curious as Don Gaspar to find out if Doña Amalia was whoring around or not, and why she had bought all that fancy underwear if she wasn't going to use it with her husband. Life, after all, was one part curiosity and one part commitment. The commitment part came in making sure Don Gaspar didn't beat up his wife. Hector figured everybody had the right to screw around a little now and then, as long as they didn't hurt anybody else too much. He picked up the ten thousand pesos Carlos had left him. If the old lady was innocent, he'd take the money and buy her a whole bunch of brassieres, garter belts, and panties in all the colors of the rainbow.

He stuck the money in his pocket and went over to the office safe. He got out his gun and shoulder holster and put them on. Then he signed a fake autograph on the Valenzuela poster on the wall, dedicating it to his other officemate, Gilberto Gómez Letras, and headed out for the hospital.

It was raining. It was the end of February and it was raining already. Every day the city became more hostile toward its children. During the bus ride Hector listened to a pair of passengers talking about the different kinds of viruses in the air: mutant viruses all around them in the smog-filled Mexico City air, the thick rain that stained your clothes when you hung them out on the roof top to dry. He raised his jacket collar and weaved his way through the puddles. The city was saying hello, the same as always. It had been waiting for him. Tough as ever, although maybe not that much tougher than a lot of the people who lived there. Hector misjudged his step and came down flush in the middle of a big puddle. He couldn't help but smile. The city was welcoming him home.

Anita lay in her hospital bed. The television was on, but she wasn't listening; she was ignoring the faces that flashed across the screen. It was only on so that she wouldn't have to spend too much time alone with herself. It was a familiar relationship for Hector: woman–television set. He'd seen it before, when his father had taken sick for the last time. A motor oil ad boomed into the room, distracting him, but he knew enough not to turn off the set.

Anita looked vulnerable, lying there. Her pale arms stretched out over the too-white sheets. Bruises on one arm above the wrist. Her chin swollen and sutured. Her combed-out red hair streaming across the pillow. The picture was perfect, irresistible, anguished. Without hesitation, Hector added himself to the list of Anita's admirers and protectors. Elisa had told him how they'd beat her with brass knuckles, raped her, and then left her bleeding in the street on another rainy day like this one.

"What's up, Red? You look like you're straight out of 'General Hospital,' " he said, taking his eyes away from the window, the fat drops falling and breaking against the glass.

"So you're my detective. Who would've guessed? You always used to be such a brat."

"No, I was just older and you looked up to me."

"What else could I do? I was only about five-three back then."

"And now?"

"Now I'm probably not even five feet, after what they did to me."

She started to cry, big tears that could have turned the rain green with envy.

"Come on, you don't need to do that."

Anita kept on crying, unembarrassed, without trying to hide her face, immobile, her hands still at her sides.

Hector shot an angry glance at the TV with his good eye and banged his fist two or three times into the bathroom door.

He needed the right dose of curiosity to draw him into a story. But he needed *them,* the others, to help him finish it off, pushing him along to the bloody end. That or a good pinch of hatred to chew between his teeth. And now he had it. If he ever found the men who'd hurt Anita he was going to squeeze their heads until the shit came out their ears.

Anita watched him through her tears and Hector watched back. They stayed that way for several seconds. Not out of any particular sense of melodrama. Not because the abused woman's pale green eyes continued to feed his new-found hatred. Hector just didn't know what else to do.

"Sit down," Anita said. Her voice sounded like she was dying.

Hector looked around for a chair, but the only one was taken up by a vase of faded roses. And the window sill, where the rain dappled melodically, was too narrow to sit on.

"Don't worry, I won't bite," she said, the beginnings of a smile growing in her teary eyes.

Hector went over to the bed, stroked the young woman's face with a hand he knew was too dry to transmit the affection he felt.

Anita moved her arms for the first time since Hector had walked into the room, motioning for him to sit by her side on the bed.

"Now you know how it feels."

Hector nodded.

"You're the only one I'm going to tell this to, Hector. I told Elisa some of it, but I couldn't . . . it's too much. So I'm going to tell you the whole thing, get it out . . . and then I'm going to try and forget all about it. Forever. It already feels like it wasn't me, like it happened to somebody else. And it was only two weeks ago. . . . They were inside my hotel room when I got there. When I opened the door they grabbed me. It was dark, but I could see them with the light from the street. The first guy, the one who grabbed me, pulled me by the hair across the room. I mean he really pulled me. When they found me later on the doctor said I was bleeding from the roots of my hair. . . . They yanked me across the room. They said I was a fucking bitch and to get the hell out of Mexico. That's all they ever said. One of them turned on the lamp by the bed. I screamed. But then this other one, who'd been sitting in a chair, he got up and hit me in the face with one of those things in his hand—what do you call them, brass knuckles. Oh, Hector, you don't know. . . . I screamed and screamed, and I can't believe that no one heard me. I screamed until I couldn't scream any more. I was too scared to talk. I felt like I was going to die, I couldn't breathe. The first guy, the one who pulled me by the hair—he was blond, with acne all over his face—he threw me on the floor. Then the one with the brass knuckle thing kicked me. I could feel my ribs break. It's strange, but that actually helped somehow, it made it so I could breathe again. He was strong, really strong, he had big muscles. Like Chelo. Do you remember Chelo, your neighbor's old chauffeur back at the house in Coyoacán? Like that, short, stocky, with black curly hair, dressed real fancy, with this checkered sport coat and a thick mustache. He kicked me in the ribs and then yelled at me to quit screaming. But I'd already stopped, it was all I could do just to keep breathing. Then the blond guy started to pull off my clothes, he just tore them off. When they raped me I still had little pieces of my clothes on, my belt, my socks, one shoe. I don't know why I remember things like that. And they both yelled at me the whole time. Not the third one, though. He didn't say anything until the end, when he told me I had to get out of Mexico. He said I had enough money already and that if I wanted to stay alive I'd better get the hell away from here. They had a bunch of papers, whole stacks of them, and they sat me down at the desk, in front of the mirror, and they put a pen in my hand and told me to sign or they'd kill me. Sign or you're dead, bitch, like that. So I looked at myself in the mirror and I signed, but with a fake name, not with my own. And not because I was being brave or anything. It's just that I couldn't remember what my name was. It was like I'd forgotten who I was. And all I could think about was revenge, getting back at them somehow, the three of them, whoever they were. To hurt them like they'd hurt me. . . . After I'd signed the papers the third one made a phone call, said something like, 'Okay, it's all taken care of,' then it was like he was listening to someone for a while. And then the blond guy, the one with the acne, took out a knife and stabbed me in the leg and I started to scream again, and then he threw me back down on the floor and he stuck . . . he stuck my bra in my mouth so that I couldn't scream anymore. And my bra was all bloody, I could taste it. That's all I remember. They went away; I wanted them to go away, and they went away. When I woke up, I was out in the street. These two paperboys found me, it was raining, and then I remember the lights from the ambulance, but I didn't hear a thing."

Anita stopped talking and looked out the window.

"You got it out. Now you can forget about it," said Hector.

"No, I can't forget."

"Sure you can. Give it another week and you'll be just fine. As soon as they let you out of here I'll take you dancing."

"You don't even know how to dance."

"I've got a week to learn."

"I'm scared, Hector."

"Why don't you go away?"

"Where to? New York? To the place where Luis died? There's nowhere else I've got. And with who? Who's going to go with me?" asked Anita, the tears coming back to her eyes. "I'm alone a lot here. Sometimes Elisa comes to keep me company, but I'm afraid they'll do something to her too. . . . You know, it was raining when they found me, I was completely soaked, and I didn't even know it."

"I'm going to bring you the best pair of baby-sitters you've ever had. You've got nothing to worry about. As long as you stay here, you'll be all right. How much money have you got?"

"Plenty. I was in the middle of fixing up things with the inheritance. The lawyer put five million pesos in my account."

"Write me a check for fifty thousand."

"With the right signature this time?"

"That's right."

"What's it for?"

"Your new bodyguards."

"What about you?"

"My services are free. You just tell me what you want me to do."

"I want to know what's going on. I want to know who killed Luis and his brothers, who did this to me."

"We're going to do more than just find out what happened," said Hector. Suddenly he felt arrogant and cheap. But he didn't take back what he'd said. He turned to look at the rain out the window. "Can you ask them to put another bed in here? I'm going to sleep here tonight."

Anita nodded.

"Anita, you awake?" asked Hector in the darkness.

"Yes. Do you want me to turn on the light?"

"No, that's okay. . . . What were the three brothers like?"

"The oldest one, Pancho, the one they shot to death, was a pathetic sort of asshole. It feels awful to say it now that he's dead, but I said it to his face more than once when he was alive. He talked about people like they were things. His car, his friends, his waiter, his chauffeur, his desk, his airplane ticket. He studied architecture for a while, but he flunked more classes than he passed. He was always a real joker, too proud for his own good, a fancy dresser, and a real mama's boy, although in this case it was with his father. The mother died I don't know how long ago. I always thought the old man had another house somewhere, because every now and then he'd disappear without telling anyone where he'd gone to. The family was from Guadalajara, at least that's where Luis's mom was from. The old man started out managing one of those big department stores, Salinas and Rocha, or Palacio de Hierro, I don't know which, and that's where he met his wife. Luis never talked about her. He didn't remember her very well. Luis was a wonderful man, always in a good mood, always ready to do something for somebody else. He never got along very well with his father or Pancho. He was the middle brother. He was only thirty years old. We got married two years ago and went to the United States to study. To tell you the truth, we went because Luis wanted to get away from his family. They were a bunch of assholes, I really mean it. . . . I don't even want their money. How did I get mixed up in this?"

"What about the younger brother, the one who's in the mental institution?"

"Alberto was the dumb one. He wanted to run a nursery and sell flowers, like Matsumoto. I always thought maybe he was gay. He was shy. He would spend hours sitting in front of the television set. He was a good driver and he used to drive his dad around a lot, as his chauffeur. He kept dropping out of school. He wasn't a bad sort of person, really, it just didn't always seem like he was playing with a full deck."

"Did Luis ever say anything about his father's business?"

"I knew that he had a bunch of furniture stores. But Luis didn't know any more than I did. When he got that letter from the lawyer, when we were back in New York, I swear his eyes nearly popped out of his head. He couldn't believe it. He thought there was some mistake, he never knew his dad had anywhere near that much money. That's all I know. Believe me, I've spent hours and hours trying to think of something, trying to remember something that might help. Anything. Some friend of the old man's I might have met sometime, something he might have said, something Luis would have told me. But there's nothing. I swear it, I can't think of a thing."

"Where's their house?"

"Here in town, in Polanco. They had a maid. I tried to find her when we came back to Mexico, but she'd disappeared. Elisa went and got my things out of the hotel, she can give you the keys to the house."

"Do you know anything else about the maid?"

"They called her Doña Concha, she'd been with them for years and years. She was the one who raised the boys, really. I think everything that happened was too much of a shock for her. The police questioned her, but it turned out that the day Pancho was killed was her day off and she wasn't around. Luis talked to her, too, but he didn't find out anything either. I don't think she had anything to do with it. Who knows where she's gone to now."

"Did you try and talk to Alberto?"

"We went to see him in the hospital. He won't talk, it's like he doesn't even see anything. Luis tried to bring him out of it, but finally the doctors told him to stop, they said he was just upsetting him unnecessarily. They said he was gone and wasn't coming back. Hell, I've got to remember to send a check to the hospital. . . ."

Hector was silent. He'd run out of questions. After a while he lit a cigarette. A light flashed momentarily over Anita's bed as well.

"You know what, Hector?"

"What?"

"The whole thing's been like a nightmare. A nightmare's the same way: weird, senseless, terrifying."

Hector nodded, but Anita couldn't see him.

IV

THE RAT'S STORY, AS FAR AS HECTOR
KNEW IT, AND A FEW OTHER THINGS HE
DIDN'T KNOW

Maybe it was just because Hector never turned around to look at his classmates in the back row, or maybe there was simply nothing to call his attention to the fish-faced kid in the blue or gray hand-me-down suits that hung loosely off his shoulders. Maybe it was because Melgar never opened his mouth in class, didn't really seem to belong there. The fact was that in that third dull year of engineering school, when the two of them shared the same classes, Hector barely even noticed that Arturo Melgar existed. At least not until the end of the year, when three weeks before exams, after asking the professor's permission, the candidates of the Self-Improvement Slate filed across the front of the classroom. Melgar came at the end of the line, with his sad puppy-dog face and fish eyes behind thick dark lenses which he only took off once, to mop up the sweat that ran off his forehead. Hector and his classmates recognized the boy from the back row. But it was all the same to them. The Self-Improvement Slate sponsored a school-wide dance and went on to win over an uninspired CP slate whose rhetoric about university democracy rang hollow in those years of student apathy. So Melgar flunked his classes and passed on to politics.

That was the last time the two of them shared classes or lab time and, for Hector, Melgar became just another obscure footnote from the past. Part of the crowd that used to hang out and get drunk in front of the east wing of the main faculty building. Parading around campus in a flashy new suit and tie, just for the sake of being seen. Slowly Melgar started to take on an air of authority. Now and then Hector heard rumors about his strange exploits: how he'd led a gang of thugs in an assault on the School of Sciences building to stop a showing of Fellini's *8½;* how he sold grass on campus, not a very common thing back then before the student movement of '68, when a couple of bennies and a glass of rum was still the biggest thrill around. People said Melgar was paid for his services by someone in the dean's office (although it was never very clear exactly what those services were, beyond the rumored ties to the growing university mafia).

In the days before the student movement, Melgar acquired a certain notoriety. Everybody was already calling him "The Rat" by then, and his name climbed several points in the always erratic campus popularity ratings. There were all kinds of rumors: they said he'd organized a student strike in a high school that ended with the firing of the principal; they said he was on the payroll of the PRI, the government party; they said he ran an extortion racket on the *colectivo* drivers whose routes crossed the university; they said he carried a gun and a knife everywhere he went.

Hector remembered seeing him twice. Once, in a student assembly where he was heckled out of the hall, only to come back half an hour later with a gang of friends, tossing ammonia bombs into the crowd. The other time, which was the one he remembered best after all those years, came when Hector was walking across the green zone in back of the campus, thinking about what a mess everything had become, how something had gotten lost, broken, and how maybe if he bought some flowers for a girl named Marisa everything would be okay again. The Rat was lying on the grass, his broken glasses next to his clenched fist. Looking at Hector without seeing him, fat tears rolling down his cheeks. Hector helped him stand up. "Thanks, bro, I owe you one," said The Rat, wiping the snot from his nose. Hector didn't say anything, just helped him walk to the edge of campus where The Rat pulled brusquely away from him. No matter how hard he tried, years later, Hector couldn't remember Marisa's face, but The Rat's myopic stare and his fat tears came back to him like yesterday.

Every Christmas for the next two or three years a giant basket of fruit arrived at Hector's door, accompanied by a simple card that said only: Arturo Melgar. Elisa used to tease him about his dubious friendship with the student gang leader.

Hector never saw The Rat again, outside of an occasional newspaper photo. The first time was when he'd tried to break up a student demonstration in '68 and someone had shot him through the liver. The second time there was a prison number across The Rat's chest. He was accused of organizing a band of urban guerrillas! Each time, Hector put the paper aside and thought, for a few seconds, about how life in Mexico was a mystery worthy of its own rosary.

That was The Rat's story as far as Hector knew it, and although in itself it was an acceptable summary of the man's remarkable biography, it barely scratched the surface of the intricate political alliances which Arturo Melgar had managed to form during those turbulent years.

What Hector didn't know was that by the time The Rat was twenty years old he'd discovered a political modus operandi through which risks and loyalties carried him along an erratic path toward the center of power. He'd learned to play a game in which the rules changed constantly, where the players changed their skins, kissed ass, trampled on the law, accumulating a kind of personal power which gave them the freedom to operate, to negotiate, and to sell themselves to the highest bidder.

At the start he'd offered up his loyalty and anti-Communist zeal to the university authorities, but his intuition and his friends told him it wasn't a good idea to serve only one master, unless he wanted to end up as a bureaucrat lost in an office somewhere or as somebody's errand boy. He set up a petty extortion racket, preying on the street vendors on the west side of the campus. He learned to be both strong and servile, despotic and obedient, cruel and brave. His balls were his biggest commodity. He learned to be a smooth talker, he learned to deal, he found his place as the intermediary between the buyers of certain services and the Neanderthal thugs who provided those services, he became a leader, learning what it took to hold a gang together.

Little by little, he rose up through the underground of small-time punks, establishing contacts with the ultimate source of power, the physical manifestation of the Mexican state, nebulous as it was before his myopic eyes: Federal District functionaries, a top university official, south side party bosses, police commanders.

He stuck to what he'd learned: serve everyone but depend on no one. His dope sales brought in the cash he needed to assert his control over the university gangs. And the authorities turned a blind eye in exchange for services rendered.

The rise of the university Left after 1966 gave The Rat plenty to do: disrupting student elections, crashing movie showings, breaking strikes, selling information, inciting riots, playing one group off against another, kidnapping professors. And along the way he managed to find the time for a little free-lancing, stealing a hundred typewriters from the university storeroom, setting up a whorehouse near the Desierto de los Leones.

The Rat achieved an ephemeral glory during the student movement of '68. After a private meeting with the mayor of Mexico City he became the channel through which enormous quantities of money were distributed to the different gangs hired to break the first wave of student protests. But, good intentions aside, there was little The Rat could do against a movement that brought hundreds of thousands of students out into the streets. He broke up one student assembly, vandalized a parking lot full of cars during a demonstration, and fed information to the police, who already had more than they knew what to do with. The Rat got desperate. In September he tried to break up a demonstration at the Polytechnic. But somebody shot him as he forced his way up to the microphone with a piece of re-bar in his hand.

Abandoned by friends and enemies alike, The Rat sat out the final months of the movement in a private hospital in Toluca. He was twenty-eight years old and alone. But by the time the student gangs surfaced again in 1969, The Rat had moved on. He'd been given a special mission by the federal police: to organize an urban guerrilla cell. The Rat had hit the big time and he kissed his student days good-bye. Now he had money to burn. Especially after pulling off a pair of bank robberies as part of his cover. He had an arsenal of machine guns and small-caliber weapons, safe houses, and a newly acquired leftist vocabulary that helped him recruit a handful of lost souls. They carried out three operations in all (the two bank robberies and the kidnapping of a politician, all with the blessings of the police). He recruited sixteen men, eleven of whom he sent out on a suicide mission from which they never returned. But then there was a change of policy in the upper echelons of the police department, and The Rat's guerrilla cell was crushed by the same people who had created it. A surprise attack, lots of press coverage, hundreds of policemen and soldiers. For one brief moment The Rat forgot who he was working for, but all his stubbornness got him was a rifle butt to the mouth. He spent six months in Lecumberri prison, during which his salary was faithfully deposited in his bank account, and he walked out of jail with a lot less noise than when he went in.

It was 1972 and the profit had gone out of the university racket. The Rat scrounged around in the garbage dump of his memory, trying to remember where he'd seen the gold shining through. He got together with a few of his old friends and set up a bodyguard service for lower-level politicians and bureaucrats. He invested some money in condominiums and dabbled briefly in the sale of hard drugs, but he got out fast. He was infringing on the big boys' territory and he could see that if he kept it up he was going to get his fingers burned. Then it came time for elections and a new administration in Mexico City and The Rat wormed his way back into the game. To his credit, he specialized in working inside the system while always keeping one foot on the outside. It was both a little more lucrative and a little more risky.

In the mid-seventies, The Rat found his gold mine. And he started to empty it.

"It's not often you get to hear what you want on the radio. You just turn it on and take what comes. That's what this business is like."

—*Luis Hernández*

"**H**ow do I look? Do I look all right? Well, I'm not. It's all a front. I'm scared shitless. Pardon the expression. I've barely slept in a week. Everywhere I go, I'm always looking over my shoulder to see if anyone's following me. I didn't want to have anything to do with this in the first place. I don't want to know anymore. I was Mr. Costa's lawyer. As far as I knew, all the old guy ever had was a couple of crummy furniture stores. I never knew anything about the rest of that shit, and I don't want to know anything about it now. I did what I had to do. I made sure that all the money that was supposed to got into his daughter-in-law's bank account. That's as far as it goes. I don't have anything to do with it anymore.''

Hector stared the lawyer in the face. The lawyer fidgeted around in his chair while he talked, his hands shook, his eyebrows twitched, he kept shifting his feet, scratching his armpits.

"I don't think we understand each other," said Hector. "I'm not asking you to do anything new. I don't want to make any trouble for you. All I want is for you to tell me who gave you the message, and exactly what they said. Exactly, so that I can be sure."

"Look, I already told the girl. Now they're going to think I told you. . . ." His words floated in the air. A diploma hung on the wall, vintage 1960, with a picture of a younger version of the same lawyer trying to hide the shit he already was behind the infantile grin of the recent graduate.

"Just tell me what they told you," said Hector. "Who it was, and what they said. That's all I want to know and you never have to see me again."

"I don't remember," said the lawyer, scratching his chin.

Hector cleared his throat and launched a big gob of spit across the desk. He aimed for the middle of the lawyer's tie, but the man jerked back at the last second, the spit landing on the left side of his vest.

"What the fuck!"

"The message. Just tell me who it was, what they said, exactly, and how come you're so scared."

"There were two of them, a couple of punks. They stuck a gun in my face and said: 'The Rat says the money doesn't belong to the girl. Mr. Costa was just holding on to it for a while. Give her the message. Put five million in her account and leave the rest alone.' That's what they said, and that's what I told her. What the hell more do you want?"

"You no longer represent the Costa family, is that correct? Then just put all the documents in a box and send them to Vallina and Associates," said Hector, passing a small piece of paper across the desk with the accountant's address on it. He left the lawyer wiping off his vest with an expression of distaste.

After his first encounter with the city, Hector went about reintegrating himself into its rhythm in his usual way. The city moves into your body through your feet and through your eyes. So Hector walked and watched. It was the same city as always. A little more worn out maybe, a little more beat up, a little more corrupt, but still the same. He walked the boulevards, the parks, down back streets heaped with trash, he jumped fences, stopped into corner grocery stores for cigarettes and soda pop, ate tacos standing up at sidewalk stands, went into a book store and came out again with a pair of Chester Himes novels, *The History of the Conquest of the Nile,* and all the Alfred Bester books he could find. He went to the supermarket and bought two thousand pesos' worth of canned goods; wandered through Tacubaya, Colonia Escandón, Mixcoac, submerging himself in the mass of people, hallucinating with the strange combination of traffic sounds and record stores broadcasting *cumbias* into the street. He walked and watched until his feet cooked inside his shoes and his good eye started to tear. By the time he gave up, he figured the city had taken him back in as one of its own. Mexico City, it wasn't the most hospitable place in the world but, if there was anyplace he could call home, this was it.

His reentry complete, the nostalgia he felt for the last lonely palm tree on the beach evaporated into the dirty air. He was ready.

When he got to the office he kicked off his shoes and stretched out in the worn-out old armchair. It looked like Carlos the upholsterer had decided that the lilac love seat wasn't worth the effort; he'd left it there to decay with time, an absurd ruin, its guts running over the sides and the springs popping out at strange angles.

He lit a cigarette; it started to rain. The wind shook the window, accompanying the rumble of his thoughts.

It all seemed simple enough. It was dirty money, bad money, and The Rat had some kind of stake in it.

So it seemed pretty obvious that The Rat was behind the murder of the Costa brothers, to keep them from getting their hands on the money, undoubtedly amassed without honest sweat, accumulated through bribes, scams, double-dealing, corruption, and blood. According to the rules of the game the money belonged to The Rat . . . to him, or to one of his many employers sunk in the sewers of power. . . . So why get involved? To protect Anita, to get her out of the mess she was in, to get her the hell away from all that trash. For the first time in a long time his curiosity wasn't there to push him along. He didn't feel that thirst for vengeance either, for vengeance in the name of the dead, in the name of the living, for the sake of what he thought this country ought to be, something he'd felt so many times before. The most he felt was a desire to destroy the men who'd raped Anita, pawns in someone else's game, rotten pieces in a putrid machine. If he wanted to, he could dive in, dig around in the crap, stir things up, uncover who knows how much fraud, corruption, bad deals, piles of money. But where was it going to get him? Chances were he was going to end up sacrificing a good piece of flesh somewhere along the line, or all of it, down to the bone; chances were he was going to get turned from the hunter into the hunted so fast he wouldn't know what hit him. Sooner or later some big fat finger would point him out in the crowd. Was that what he wanted? He knew that when he got to the end, if he even made it that far, he'd come up against a wall standing between himself and justice. A wall of situations, alibis, connections, guns, desks, brute force, habits, and complicities that stretched from the deepest corner of the criminal underground to the heights of power. Carlos, his brother, could have told him the same thing. Only, if Carlos were saying it, Hector would have come to another set of conclusions, he'd have found other answers, or the absence of answers, and an inertia that would carry him on to the end. And then Carlos would explain to him that it wasn't really the end, that all he'd done was dig a little bit of dirt out from under the fingernails of power. Hector felt tired. You can't start a war you know you're going to lose. But what else could Hector do? There was nowhere for him to go, no place, no thing, no home sweet home, no habits to lose himself in. So he walked in his stocking feet across the splintery trash-covered floor and picked up the telephone. He'd get Anita her pair of bodyguards, then make the other couple of calls that were sure to propel him on into this story that, without wanting to, he was going to make his own.

"What do you think about your new baby-sitters?" he asked the woman sunk down under the covers, holding the door open for El Angel II and El Horrores. The big men had seen better days, their faces scarred, their professional wrestlers' reflexes dulled, their step now slack. There wasn't any ring that would take them any-more but, even so, their gigantic bulk, their hardened faces, the muscles bulging through their jackets, their enormous hands, compelled respect.

"Anita, I want you to meet a couple of friends of mine, El Angel II and El Horrores. El Angel was heavyweight wrestling champ for six months back in 1962 . . ."

"It was only five months, miss."

". . . and El Horrores once beat Blue Demon with his patented spinecruncher hold." El Horrores and El Angel put on their best smiles. Anita didn't know whether to hide herself under the sheets or ask the two wrestlers—they must have weighed nearly five hundred pounds be-tween them—to sing her a lullaby.

"With these two here, nobody's going to get through this door unless you say so. Take my word for it," said Hector. He was amused by the contrast between the fragile, diminutive redhead and his two towering friends, who, feeling a little bit intimidated, edged into a corner of the room and tried their best to become invisible.

"And besides, they can play cards and dominoes, and

El Angel's not a bad chess player." The big man grinned at Anita, chunks of gold and silver showing where his teeth used to be. Anita tried a weak smile.

"Mr. Angel, Mister . . ."

"Just call me Horrores, miss."

"I guess I only know how to play canasta, and I'm not very good at it, either. . . ."

"We'll learn, miss, don't you worry," said El Horrores. Things were already turning out better than he'd hoped.

Hector leveled an appraising glance at his team of caretakers and nodded with pride. If he ever had the chance, he could put together the most original cast of characters that any detective novel ever had.

He had to move fast, make up for the time he'd wasted. Half an hour later he stepped into the main offices of Vallina and Associates, Accountants, stared in greeting at Vallina-and-Associates-Accountants (which, like God, was merely a single individual with a triple identity), and asked if he'd finished his review of the Costa family's financial records.

Vallina handed a folder across his desk. The elbows of his suit shone with wear. There was a photograph on the office wall showing him standing next to the Queen of England (while the Queen was real enough, the man in the photo was only somebody who looked like him).

"I whipped it off for you in two hours, Hector. That makes us six to four."

"In your favor or mine?"

"Who are you kidding, Hector? Mine, of course."

"I guess I owe you two, then."

Vallina nodded, took out a handkerchief, and blew his nose enthusiastically. Little bits of snot hung onto his mustache. Despite his best efforts, Vallina had never quite grasped the secrets of success in the capitalist system. All he could do now was wait for the revolution for his chance to get ahead in this world.

"How about if I collect them both at once?" he asked. "I've got a couple of things I need you to look into for me."

Hector walked over to a small refrigerator in a corner of the room.

"How about if we make it another time? This case I'm working on now has me full up. And I've already got another one. I can't exactly go around like some amateur trying to cover six jobs all at once."

The light in the refrigerator was burned out. There was half a chorizo and an open bottle of flat soda pop. Hector shook the bottle to test its age and took a cautious sip.

Vallina made a noise in his throat. "As if this job wasn't crazy enough for you," he said. He undid one of the buttons of his dress shirt and scratched his belly through the T-shirt underneath.

"This other one's just your kind of thing, too. The case of the colored underwear. Speaking of which, is that a Dallas Cowboys T-shirt you're wearing?"

"How'd you know?"

Hector tucked the envelope Vallina had given him under his arm. Despite his outward sloppiness, the accountant's work was careful and precise, accurate down to the minutest detail.

"I owe you two," said Hector, and he went out the office door.

Belascoarán found a seat in the back row of a lecture by the lawyer Hector Mercado about "The Origins of Article 123 of the Constitution" at the Reforma Cultural Center. Ignoring the lawyer's talk, he read through Vallina's cramped three-page typed report. His choice of a substitute office space was no accident. Once he got started on a case it was essential that he break with his routines, to keep himself from being turned into a sitting duck. If he was going to become somebody's target—which, under the circumstances, wasn't at all unlikely—he was going to be a moving target, like the character in a Ross Macdonald novel he'd once read. A moving target, weaving and bobbing, unpredictable as only an inhabitant of this huge city could be with a little bit of imagination.

While the lawyer rattled on about the Constitutional Convention of 1917, Hector lost himself in Vallina's account of Old Man Costa's finances. The pages were full of question marks where the accountant had lacked sufficient data to back up his conclusions, but the story held together well enough.

Starting in August 1977 the already well-to-do furniture merchant had begun to move quantities of cash ten to twenty times the amount he'd dealt in before, investing the money in the most varied places. It almost seemed like his biggest problem was just figuring out what to do with it all. According to Vallina, there was no real pattern, no strategy, in the crazy hodgepodge of investments. The old man had started out thinking like a furniture merchant, investing the money in stores and boutiques, small businesses with small profits, nothing very exciting. Later on he went into gold, silver, jewels. He bought up part of a small commercial airline, two fishing boats, a bottling plant. He always worked alone, never took on partners. And he reinvested the profits from this growing network of investments almost immediately. Pretty soon he'd accumulated over two hundred million pesos in cash, gold, silver, jewels, and business investments.

It was clear enough that the old man's heart attack was a direct result of having to manage a bizarre mini-empire that included everything from a candy store in downtown Mexico City to fifteen million pesos in gold coins in a safe deposit box in Monterrey.

"Where's the master account book?" Vallina had written in one of the margins. He'd had to reconstruct everything from fragments, notarized contracts, sales receipts, scraps of paper.

Another note at the end indicated that in 1977 and 1978 Costa had cheated the government out of millions of pesos in taxes.

It was dirty money, that was obvious enough. But where had it come from? Whose was it? New money came in often enough, but without any regularity, and in amounts that varied from one to ten million pesos at a time. His choice of cities and states followed a clear pattern: Guadalajara, Monterrey, the northwestern states, Puebla. All eighteen of his businesses outside Mexico City fell into one of these four areas. And he'd pretty much divided the money equally between cash, business investments, and precious metals and jewels. That seemed to be the old man's way of covering himself against losses.

There was one last detail: money went in, but it didn't go out. Whoever had used Costa as a banker hadn't made any withdrawals.

The trip to Cuernavaca was pointless; Hector had known it before he even started out. He'd just wanted to see Alberto Costa's face, and he'd seen it. The detective and the youngest of the three Costa brothers sat staring silently at each other for fifteen minutes. Hector smoked a couple of cigarettes, chatted briefly with the doctor, and left the asylum. He took a taxi to the bus station and then took the hour-long bus ride back to the city. He hadn't found anything he could bring back with him. Not even a feeling of sympathy, just a sense of emptiness, distances. Alberto was somewhere else and Hector had no way of knowing whether that somewhere else was any better or any worse than the world the twenty-five-year-old boy had left behind.

It was getting dark when he got back to Mexico City. He got in a cab and gave a couple of fake addresses before he worked himself up to asking the driver to leave him in front of a building in the Colonia Nápoles. He rang the bell several times and was just starting to think about where he was going to spend the night when the super, returning home with a bagful of fresh pastries, let him in, gave him a smile, and handed him a note with his name on it.

"The young lady's gone off to Tequesquitengo. Been there about a month now, water skiing. She left this note for you. You are Hector, aren't you? Why, of course you are, I just forget so easily," she said.

The note wasn't much: "We're even. Nobody's there when you're looking for them. You taught me that. Remember? Me."

On the other side of the piece of paper he wrote an even shorter reply: "Don't even think that I came by. Me." He put it back in the envelope and handed it to the super, who sensed his disappointment.

But it wasn't even really disappointment that he felt. It was just plain basic ugly loneliness. With a half-smile hovering around the edges, because that's how the game was played. Sometimes there was a shoulder to cry on and sometimes there wasn't. And if you weren't around to offer your shoulder when it was your turn, the shoulder wouldn't be there when you needed it, either. That's just the way it was.

Without realizing what he was doing, Hector found himself on a minibus that left him off half a dozen blocks from his house. He ignored his own warnings to himself not to do anything stupid, and headed for home. The sky was black by the time he opened the door to his apartment.

The layer of dust wasn't all that thick. The place wasn't as desolate as he'd imagined. He almost felt cheated. After seven months away his apartment should have been a complete wreck. But that's not how it was, the place was a lot worse when he lived there. There weren't any dirty clothes lying around on the floor, his books and records were more or less where they ought to be, the dust was evenly distributed—not piled up in anarchic clumps from ashtrays full of cigarette butts he'd spilled as he walked to the door half asleep to open up for the milkman or the garbage man. Even his bed was made. What the hell was going on? It had been four years since the last time his bed had been made.

Feeling like a ghost, he picked up the telephone. A recording told him that his line had been disconnected. The phone company was getting friendlier all the time, informing their delinquent customers, and not just outside callers, that their service had been cut off. It was doubly considerate really, because it gave you the option of talking with the voice on the recording, if you were quick enough to get the words out in the right places.

"*We are sorry to inform you*—Baby! How's it going? It's been a long—*orarily out of service*—Out of service your ass, sweetheart—*(silence)* . . . *We are sorry*—Never say you're sorry, baby. . . ."

He hung up. That's not what craziness was all about. Craziness was more sophisticated than that, like fixing dinner for two when you live alone.

He was setting the plates out on the table when the doorbell rang. And he was feeling so good that he opened the door for his potential murderers with a big smile on his face. They had the looks all right, but they didn't shoot. They just grinned back and told him that an old acquaintance was waiting to see him.

VI

"It's not your fault, it's not anybody's fault. It's just the way the cards come out."

—*Doc Holliday in* Gunfight at the OK Corral, *from the screenplay by Leon Uris*

There was nothing threatening about the faces of the two bodyguards as the car followed the Circuito Interior and turned off into the labyrinthine streets of San Miguel Chapultepec. They were just carrying out the routine job of messenger-driver-gofer. Hector relaxed, his arm pressed tight against the gun at his side. The car pulled up in front of a vacant lot. The driver and his partner got out and waited for Hector to crawl out of the backseat. Then, without even looking back to see if he was following, they crossed the empty lot, under the light of a solitary lamppost, to a building with a metal staircase spiraling up the three stories to the roof. A man about fifty years old was waiting at the top of the stairs. He searched Hector clumsily and took away his gun while the two thugs watched without interest.

"I'll hold onto this for you, sonny," he said in a friendly voice and, tossing the gun onto a rain-rusted metal chair, erased Hector from his mind. The driver guided Belascoarán past the empty cages for hanging out the wash, the tanks of gas, pushed open a metal door, and they went inside. They headed down a wooden stairway that widened out at the second floor, where bad reproductions of Modiglianis and van Goghs hung on the walls, and finally brought them to a large living room on the ground floor, all the furniture covered with white sheets and an abandoned smell in the air. A uniformed servant carrying a tray loaded with plates and glasses came out of a swinging door that seemed to lead to the kitchen. The driver pointed Hector to an armchair.

"Make yourself comfortable. The boss'll see you in a minute."

Hector settled into the sheet-covered chair and waited.

"Come in, Mr. Belascoarán," said The Rat's voice from behind a sliding door. Hector stood up and pushed the door open. The room was almost dark, with a metal desk in the center full of newspaper clippings, receipts, sheets of stationery with the PRI letterhead, scribbled-on file cards, and behind it, in an executive-style leather swivel chair, The Rat. Oddly enough, there was no telephone on the desk.

"Have a seat, bro. Please," said The Rat, whose myopia had increased from what Hector remembered to the point where his glasses were two dense lenses mounted in black plastic frames. His features had become more marked, his jaw hung slightly, his nose sloped forward, his uncombed hair spread out thinly on top of his head. He was clean-shaven, but he'd let his sideburns grow down longer than was currently stylish. The overall impression was that of a sickly and childlike adult.

"I'd pretty much forgotten all about you, you know. We were in the same class, weren't we? In engineering."

Hector nodded.

"I knew it; that weird name of yours isn't too easy to forget. And you finished, didn't you? You graduated. Sure, of course you did, how were you going to drop out? You were always one of the good ones, the brains. Those were the days, weren't they? But that's all water under the bridge now, isn't it?"

Hector nodded again.

"I had you sent for," said The Rat, staring off in another direction, maybe imagining the street that must have been out there beyond the drawn curtain, " 'cause I said to myself, this Belascoarán's got to be my old buddy, my . . . But then I thought, no, that'd be too much of a coincidence. But now here you are. I think we're going to understand each other real good. Aren't we, bro?"

Hector nodded.

The Rat stopped talking, waiting for an answer from Hector, or from the inner voice that must have talked to him at night, scolding him for his sins, congratulating him for his successes, or just advising him on proper table manners, personal hygiene, and nutrition. The real sons of bitches always have an inner voice they can count on to give them a hand when they need it.

Finally he said, "You just tell the girl that the money's not hers. Tell her the money didn't belong to the old guy or his kids either. . . . Tell her that he—how should I put it?—he was just holding on to it for safe keeping. You got that? Look at it this way, bro: if you're a banker you don't get to keep the money in the accounts, do you? That's just basic economics. We gave her her share— more than her share if you ask me. We've been more than generous with her, but that's okay, we'll just call it service charges, like in a bank. Understand? We'll just call it that, all right, bro?''

"Call it whatever the hell you want. What happens now?''

"Now? Nothing. That's the end of the story. She keeps her share and leaves the rest alone. I'll take care of it, she doesn't have to worry about a thing. We'll fix it all through her lawyer, no problems, no taxes, everything nice and clean.''

"And the dead brothers?'' said Hector, looking straight at The Rat.

"What're you worried about, the money or the dead? Because here in Mexico, bro, it's either one or the other—my money or my dear departed who I've got to avenge, who I've got to settle accounts for. They kill so many of mine, I kill so many of theirs, and I even up the score. And that's that. But what do you care, anyway? These ones, they died stupid, see? The old man, he even died of natural causes. . . . I didn't have anything to do with it, besides. They're not my dead. I'm not going to take responsibility for them. You'll have to go somewhere else if you want to settle that score.''

"Where?''

"Somewhere, to someone who thinks the money belongs to him. There's always going to be someone who thinks that when a bank goes belly-up everyone's got the right to dress in black and play the part of the poor little old widow with her crummy savings account. . . ." The Rat laughed. "Fucking little old widows . . . Look, bro, get yourself out of this, it doesn't belong to you. It's not your money, it's not your old lady, it's not your bank, they're not your dead. And they're not mine either. I'll make sure the money gets taken care of, and the rest of it, too. That's what the people whose money it is pay me for, so that it all comes out nice and clean and neat, got that?"

"So who do I go to if I want to settle accounts?"

"In Mexico, bro? To the Virgin of Guadalupe." The Rat took a dirty handkerchief out of his pocket and blew his nose, very softly, as though he were afraid his body might come apart from the effort.

"Let me see if I've got this straight," said Hector, smiling. "Mr. Costa was playing banker for someone you work for who funneled Costa a shitload of dirty money. Let's call him Mr. X. Now Mr. Costa dies, and Mr. X wants his money back. Then Mr. Costa's kids die and Mr. X still wants his money, but before he can get to it Mr. Z's gone and killed Mr. Costa's kids because it turns out that Mr. X isn't the only one who wants to get his hands on the money. And now, since you work for Mr. X, you want the widow of Mr. Costa's last son to get out of Mexico and leave the money behind, but it also turns out that the people who work for Mr. Z want the widow to go away. . . ."

"Cut the crap. Since we were old classmates I invited

you over here to have a little talk. Now here's the message: You get out, she gets out. She keeps her money. Everyone's happy."

"And the dead?" said Hector, standing up.

"The dead? Which ones, bro, which ones?" said The Rat, looking at the curtains again.

Hector walked out and The Rat didn't look back in his direction. The driver was sitting outside reading a stock-car magazine. He got up to take Hector back the way they'd come.

"Fernando!" shouted The Rat from inside the office.

The driver excused himself with a nod and went in to see his boss. Hector picked up the magazine and started to read the table of contents, but The Rat's voice came clearly through the open door.

"Drop off Mr. Belascoarán wherever he wants, and then go take care of the other job I gave you. You know the one I'm talking about. But take it easy, all right? Make it look like an accident. Like something fell on him when he was out for a walk, or like a hit-and-run, a mugging, something like that. Keep it simple. I don't want you to get carried away and kill the dumbshit novelist, okay? I just want him out of circulation for a few days, a week, a month tops. Make sure you don't kill him, and I don't want it to look like someone was gunning for him either. It's got to look like an accident. No fuck-ups."

Hector wondered if The Rat had wanted him to hear his instructions on purpose, so that he'd know that he'd been forgiven, absolved by a man who had the power to kill, to destroy, a man who obeyed no law beyond the law of the jungle that this city had become.

The driver reappeared in the doorway and smiled at Hector.

"Whenever you're ready," he said.

They retraced the strange route they'd taken on the way in, Hector got his gun back, and they returned to the car where the other bodyguard waited. They got in the car and pulled away from the curb.

"Where do you want us to take you?"

"Wherever. Which way are you headed? You can just drop me off somewhere on the way."

"The boss said we were supposed to take you wherever you want," the driver answered politely.

"No, it's just that I'm not ready to go home yet. I've got a lot on my mind and I thought I'd take a walk and think things over."

"It's always that way when someone has a talk with the boss. He's always got something interesting to say, if you'll pardon my butting in," said the driver, sharing a little gangster wisdom. "We're headed over to near where we picked you up, near your house there, just one neighborhood over. In the Condesa, instead of the Roma this time."

"Hey, how about if we leave it for tomorrow, he's not going to go out this time of night," said the other gunman, ignoring Hector.

"Come on, let's get it over with. If he doesn't come out we'll just stay and wait for him."

"You want to spend all night there? We can go for him in the morning just as easy. Don't be a jerk."

The driver glanced back at Hector. "What'll it be, then?" he said over his shoulder. He drove the car along Benjamín Franklin, braking briefly at the red light at

Saltillo and accelerating to try and make the light at Nuevo León.

"Leave me here in front of the bakery on the corner."

They let him out and drove away. Hector looked around desperately for a taxi. If they didn't get too far ahead he could follow in a taxi and warn their victim about what was waiting for him. But he was out of luck. When he lost sight of the car, he went into the bakery, thumbing through his address book until he found the phone number for *Uno más uno.*

"Newsroom."

"Marciano Torres, please."

"Let me check; I think he went out."

Silence. The fluorescent streetlights glowed in the puddles outside the window, creating that phantasmagoric atmosphere that annoyed him so much. The city was unreal enough without special effects courtesy of city hall.

"Torreeees."

"Hector."

"Who?"

"Hector Belascoarán."

"What's happening, guy? It's been years. Somehow I thought you'd left us for good."

"I'm calling you because I need a favor, man, it's important. I need to know which novelists live in the Condesa and could be messed up in problems with . . . well, in problems. From some digging around they'd been doing or something."

"Shit, man, where'd you come up with this one? What do you want a novelist for? You going to tell him your life story? You'd be better off telling me. You're not exactly what I'd call novel material. You'd fit better in the crime sheet of a rag like this one. Although I don't know if I could even get you in here, man, they're kind of high-brow about that kind of stuff. You're more *La Prensa*'s kind of thing. . . . But hold on a minute, let me talk to García Junco, he knows about that literary shit. . . ."

Hector sweated out the minutes. Whoever the guy was, whether or not he'd read one of his novels, he had to get to him before The Rat's gunmen.

"The resident egghead says there're two novelists living in the Condesa, José Emilio Pacheco and Paco Ignacio, who lives on Etla. Sounds like the second one's probably your man; I guess he writes mysteries or something. I told you this wasn't your kind of thing. . . . García says he's a buddy of your brother Carlos."

Hector hung up without the obligatory "thanks, brother." Carlos's phone was busy. He dialed again.

"Carlos?"

"Do I sound like Carlos?"

"Marina!"

"Yeah. Who's this? Hector! What a surprise! Where've you been?"

"I'll tell you later. Is Carlos there?"

"He's asleep. But wait, I'll wake him up. Lately he takes his siesta from seven to nine. Do you get to trade them in for another one if you make a mistake the first time?"

"I don't know if you'd be any better off. There's always me, and I'm even worse."

"Forget it, then, I never said anything. Hold on."

Carlos's blurred voice came over the line. "Brother. What can I do you for?"

VII

"I believed that people only thought about these things in novels."

—*Nâzim Hikmet*

"So you're Carlos's brother? Come in," said the writer, holding out his hand to Hector and then breaking the handshake almost immediately, as if something else had suddenly crossed his mind.

He was more or less the same age as the detective, although they shared little in the way of appearance. The writer weighed one hundred and seventy pounds and it annoyed him to have people tell him that he was fat, maybe because he wasn't quite. He was a little under five-five, with thick hair he kept brushing back from one eye, gold-framed glasses set on top of a long nose that rested, in turn, on top of a thick, unruly mustache. When he opened the door he had a glass of Coke in one hand

and in the other, a cigarette, which he had to put in his mouth to shake Hector's hand. The glass and the cigarette hovered eternally around him, like a physical extension of his hands, and that's how Hector would always remember him. That, and a skittish pair of eyes that were always on the move, as if they were more interested in following the thread of the writer's thoughts than in focusing on his visitor's face.

"Here, have a seat," he said, walking into a room lined with bookshelves, and clearing an old sweater and a bunch of papers from a white armchair. "Carlos said you had something very important to tell me. That's how he put it, and I suppose it must be true, since Carlos doesn't usually exaggerate about that kind of thing."

Hector took a deep breath and dove directly into his story. He tried to repeat The Rat's exact words.

When he was finished, the writer offered him a cigarette from a pack of Delicado filters and pushed an empty glass, of doubtful cleanliness, toward the detective so that he could pour himself some Coke from the economy-size bottle.

"Looks like I'm screwed," he said.

"It's not that bad. You know they're after you and I know who they are. I can cover you until you can get away. Besides, The Rat made it clear that he didn't want them to hurt you too much, just take you out of circulation for a while. So if you take yourself out, that ought to satisfy them."

"Some comfort. I'm screwed either way. They obviously know what I'm on to and they're not going to let me go any further with it. If I run away, I screw myself, and if I don't, then they screw me."

"If that's the case, then we're both screwed, because they know about me now, too," said the detective with a grin. He ran his eyes over the walls full of books, trying to discover some order, some common themes, the erratic logic behind their arrangement.

"But you don't have a six-year-old daughter."

Hector looked at him. The writer hid behind an ashtray heaped with butts.

"You mean she's all yours? Where's her mother?"

"In Lisbon, the bitch. You don't write, do you? No, I didn't think so, you're more the protagonist type. . . . Well, one day I get the bright idea to fall in love with the wife of the Filipino ambassador, and, bam, I get her pregnant. The madame ambassadress—is that what you call her?—she stays holed up the whole time until she has the kid, then she leaves it with me and takes off with her cuckold husband who's been conveniently transferred to Lisbon, one big happy family."

"Does the kid live here with you? Do I get to meet her?" asked Hector.

"Of course," said the writer, and with the glass of Coke in one hand and a cigarette in the other, he led Hector along a labyrinthine hallway, lined with bookshelves like the rest of the house, to a white-painted bedroom where a girl slept in a nightgown with a teddy-bear print.

"She's a beauty, isn't she?"

"What's her name?" Hector asked, looking at the vaguely Asian face, the sleeping girl sucking on her thumb.

"Pearl Flower, like this character in a Salgari novel who was a guerrilla commander in the Philippine War. Her mother had a fit over that one. But that's the way

I wanted it and that's the way it is. We call her Spider here, in the family."

Hector and the writer returned to the other room. The writer walked over to the record player, hesitated, and went back to his chair, where he sat with his back to his desk piled with folders, photographs, books, papers, colored pens.

"What year were you born?"

"Forty-nine. You?"

"Same. February."

"Beat you. January 11; that makes me older," said the writer. "Let's have a little show of respect."

"Yes, sir." They both grinned. "Now would you mind telling me what you got yourself mixed up in that The Rat'd want to sic his dogs on you?"

"I'll trade you, Hector. You tell me your story and I'll tell you mine."

"How about some more Coke? I'll warn you ahead of time, though, my story's pretty dull. It wouldn't make a very good novel. The whole plot was pretty obvious from the beginning."

The writer went off to get another bottle of Coke and Hector glanced around the room. On the wall over one end of the desk there was a sign that read, *Never marry a woman who leaves the caps off your Magic Markers.* There were the framed covers of three crime novels, and a photograph from the Spicer strike. The nearest bookshelf held everything by Mailer, Walrauff, Dos Passos, John Reed, Carleton Beals, Rodolfo Walsh, Guillermo Thorndyke, Jim Thompson. Some of the names were familiar, others were a mystery to him. Hector promised himself to track them down someday when he had the time.

"A Coke for a story," said the writer, returning.

"A Mr. Costa, the father of three sons and the owner of a few furniture stores, dies in his sleep one day . . ." began Hector, who had the feeling he was retelling Little Red Riding Hood for the umpteenth time.

While Hector talked, the writer sat quietly, hardly moving, forcing himself not to interrupt. He smoked two cigarettes, lighting one off the other, and occasionally scratched his head. The detective tried to concentrate on his story, but part of his mind was taken up with trying to decipher his listener. It was obvious, from the tension in the writer's expression, from the way he fidgeted in his chair, that he could scarcely keep himself from interrupting.

"And that's everything there is to tell."

"Hell, it's clear as a bell. Like you said, it's dirty money, but good luck in figuring out who's behind it. Maybe The Rat's telling the truth. Maybe there's more than one of them, whoever it is he's working for and the others, the rapists and murderers. What are you going to do with it?"

"I'm going to have to talk it over with Anita, explain it to her from the beginning."

"This country's a fucking mess. Your average citizen's naked out there in the street. There's no way out."

"What about your story?"

"No, mine's more or less the same. It's just that I'm an idiot. I started out following a terrible story: fourteen bodies show up in a sewage canal. Pumped full of bullets, in their underwear, with signs of torture. Not one or two, but fourteen. The papers just print a bunch of bullshit. Then the labels in their underwear provide a clue: one of the men was wearing Venezuelan shorts. So I started to follow the story more closely. I don't know what the hell for, since I had plenty of problems on my hands to begin with. No, sure, I know why. Curiosity. Because you can never quite believe that this kind of thing's really true, even though you tell it to yourself out loud every single day. Instead of an "Our Father," the atheists in this town start off their day with: Save me, brother, from this lousy sewer that I got stuck in, protect me from all the assholes that want to fuck me over, save me from the law and its enforcers.

"You just can't quite really believe it all, no matter how much you read and how much you tell yourself, and when your luck's against you, you see it and you live it and you eat it every day. . . . So finally the mother of one of the fourteen dead men turns up, a poor, ordinary woman, she could just as well have been the old lady who sells tacos over here around the corner. She says her son was a cab driver, that he'd never had anything to do with the rest of them, the other thirteen, that he was a hard worker. And who did your son work for, ma'am? For a nice bunch of boys who rented him the taxi by the hour. Foreigners? Well, they talked a little bit like they were from Veracruz, but no, they weren't Mexican. Then the cops come out with a real doozy. They said that it was a settling of accounts between foreign guerrilla groups, Salvadorans, Colombians, in Mexico. And I say to myself, look sharp, because that's a smoke screen if there ever was one. More like a bullshit screen or a smog screen around here. So, after that, I figure it's got to be them, it's got to be the cops that're behind it all. The worst thing about it was that the dead didn't belong to anyone, they didn't even have any names. I went back over all the newspaper clippings until I found him, and said to myself: this is the one. A judicial police commander who showed up every other day piling it higher and deeper. This is the guy who killed them. All you have to do is look at his picture and you know it's got to be him. This guy probably bottle-whipped his mother to death before he was two years old. The guy's so rotten you can practically see the skin peeling off in front of your eyes. Commander Saavedra, with a ruby ring on one finger and an emerald ring on another."

"How do you know that?"

"The rings? From the color pictures in *Por Esto*. With a look of contempt on his face for the human race in general and for the nearest Mexican in particular. All I was missing was a motive, but that wasn't too hard. Colombians, drugs, coke, they were moving the stuff through Mexico to the United States. And my man finds out about it, murders them, and keeps the stuff for himself. How much could it have been worth? Two, ten, twenty million? Turning the drugs into cash isn't going to be any problem for him, the *judiciales* have the whole thing wired, that's clear as day. So I had all the pieces, all that was left to do was put them together and write my novel. Tell the story. But no, I couldn't have it be that easy, I had to know more, get some verification, see the faces, the places. And since I'm on vacation from the university, and I had some time, I went and talked to the taxi driver's mother. Then I went and checked all

the cheap hotels in town, and then the not-so-cheap hotels, and then the sort of middle range hotels, until I
found it. The hotel where they'd stayed. I went and
tracked down a couple of prostitutes who'd been friends
of the Colombians. I went to a friend in Foreign Rela-
tions to look for the names of Colombians who'd entered
the country in the month before the killings. And I found
them. I went to the Colombian embassy and spent ten
days going through the Colombian newspapers. Shit, it's
as bad there as it is here. I found a couple of them again
there. I went and found a rented car that some *judicial*
had returned late with some dumb excuse a week after
the murder, then I found a waiter who'd seen the commander talking with two of the Colombians in a restaurant out near the Toluca highway. As you can see, it was
all too easy. And that's as far as I'd gotten, when you
walk in and tell me that either I can shove it all up my
ass or wait for them to come and bust my head open."

"Where's The Rat fit in?"

"This is the first time he's made an appearance. I know
as much about him as you do. He's a messenger. An
irregular. Like the Baker Street kind. He works on the
outside for the ones on the inside."

"And your novel?"

"What novel? I'd pretty much forgotten about it by
now." The writer sat looking out through the window at
the night. "Don't you ever feel like getting the hell out
of here? Running away? Before I got involved in this
craziness I was writing an article about this buddy of
mine and a couple of his friends who got burned real
bad in this factory where they worked, and so the rest
of the workers went on strike, demanding gloves and

other safety gear, and they all ended up getting fired. It's all the same, isn't it?"

They smoked for a while in silence, each one withdrawing from the other's story to submerge himself again in his own thoughts.

"So why don't you get the hell out?"

"Why don't you?"

"Me, because I'm stubborn. And anyway, violence freaks me out, but I don't freeze up," said Hector, surprised by his own words.

"I'm not like you then, I freeze up. Everything but my asshole, that is. It gives me the runs," said the writer, proud of his confession. "I'm one chicken-shit Mexican."

"No, there isn't anyone around here who isn't scared."

"Well I get real scared. . . . You think they're out there?"

"Probably. They're driving a black Datsun with Mexico State plates."

The novelist kept his eyes fixed on the window.

"I like this street. We even get birds here in the morning. . . . There's the Datsun."

"You want to go have a little talk with them?"

"How're you going to do that?"

"Just follow me, you'll see. Have you got any gasoline?"

"What do I look like, a gas station?"

"Something that'll burn, then."

"Hell, I don't know. Maybe about half a can of lighter fluid. What're you going to do?"

"What's that Kaliman says, on the radio show?"

"*Serenity and patience, Solín.* I'm the one who's supposed to be thinking up that kind of thing, Detective."

"Leave the lights on. As long as nothing changes, they won't think anything's wrong. They're not paying any attention to people coming into the building. I walked right in behind a woman and her kid without any problem."

"That'd be Mrs. Salgado, in number three."

"But they're going to be watching for people going out. Where're they parked?"

"Just past the door, about ten or fifteen yards."

"Is there any other way out of the building?"

"No . . . wait a minute. Elías has a window that lets out on Benjamín Hill."

Belascoarán and the writer crawled through the ground-floor window of the writer's surprised neighbor and crouched motionless for an instant on the dark sidewalk.

"Wait here. Once I get them out of the car, then you can come over," said Hector, and he slipped off between the parked cars. The street was dark enough, with one lamppost at either end of the block and the light from a few windows, and it was easy for Hector to be a shadow among shadows, creeping up to the back of the Datsun. "Where's a Datsun's motor, in back or in front?" he wondered. It wouldn't do to blow up the damn thing. "In front," he decided, and, keeping out of sight of the dozing gunmen, he squirted the lighter fluid across the back of the car, more by squeezing the metal can than by dumping it out, which would have made it easier for them to see him. Then he took out his lighter and held it to a spot where he thought he'd left a good dose. The conflagration nearly blinded him for life. He fell backward from the surprise and pulled out his gun.

But if Hector thought he was surprised, the two men inside the car jumped like a pair of characters on "Sesame Street." The blazing lighter fluid gave out a bright, intense flame.

"Blow on it, maybe you can put it out," said the detective, showing the two gunmen the black hole of his .38.

"Hell, mister, this isn't fair. And I thought you were a gentleman."

"This son of a bitch is gonna fuck up our wheels," said his partner.

It made a pretty blaze, full of movement, the burning lighter fluid dripping down the car's sides.

"Put your guns on the ground and blow, I wasn't joking," said Hector. But they ignored him.

"Nice bonfire you've got there, Detective," said the writer, approaching the car and watching the two thugs out of the corner of his eye while they laid their guns on the ground, holding them delicately with two fingers as if they were covered with shit.

Just the way it had flared up, the fire died back down. A few of the neighbors clapped from the safety of their windows.

"This here's the writer you were looking for, and now he knows who you are and who you work for. So the fun's over. You'd better go tell The Rat that this is as far as it goes."

One of the rear tires started to go flat, letting out a soft hiss. Here and there the paint blistered and cracked.

"The boss isn't going to like it."

"Sorry, friend, that's how it goes sometimes," said Hector and, collecting the guns from the ground, he passed one to the writer and started back toward the apartment building.

"How'd I do?" asked Hector.

"Well, it wasn't exactly like they do it in the novels, but I'd say it was pretty damn good. One hell of a fire. I'm going to buy a couple more cans of lighter fluid, to have them around just in case."

"Buy me one, too," said Hector, grinning.

VIII

"I'm thirty years old, my hair's going grey. I'm not tired."

—*Ernst Toller*

As he moved into the fifth day of his investigation of the Costa family's destruction, Hector found himself out of sorts. Almost completely useless. What was next? He had Anita under cover in the hospital. Cautiously, he was getting back in touch with the city. He'd fixed his record player when he'd gotten home. And now, after struggling through a black night, he was at a dead end.

He'd woken up soaked with sweat, wrapped inside his sheets like a mummy, the muscles of his left arm tight and cramped, his jaw tense, his breath irregular. He'd come back to the city of his worst nightmares and, like before, he was finding it hard to wake up, a thick sleep clinging to him, dragging him down into the depths of the public and private hell of Hector Belascoarán Shayne.

He found some bottles of soda pop in the kitchen. He opened one and, trying to keep his unbuttoned pajamas from falling down, went back to bed to smoke and reconstruct his conversation with The Rat. Half an hour later he called his new friend the writer on the telephone.

"Everything okay?"

"To quote the guy who fell off a thirty-story building, when he was halfway down: so far, so good. I went out to the store and now I'm playing tic-tac-toe with my daughter. I still haven't decided what to do."

"That makes two of us."

"How's your friend in the hospital?"

"I'm going to go see her in a while."

"I think I'll write for a couple of hours and then cook up some serious food."

"Sounds good. By the way, I liked the Mailer book."

"I told you you would."

He dove into downtown Mexico City like a scuba diver into the past, repeating the same questions in the three Costa furniture stores. He was looking for a connection between the deceased owner and *someone,* prior to August 1977. Maybe an old acquaintance, a friend or client. Someone who at some point had become the link that turned Costa into a personal banker for someone who wasn't able to use the services of the Bank of Mexico. It wasn't going to be the mob, because the mob had its own system. It would have to be someone in the government, someone in a position of power, who suddenly had a huge amount of cash on his hands and no way to move it, to hold onto it. Someone who had to bury his money deep enough so that his superiors, his friends, his co-workers, the press, wouldn't know it was there. Someone who could pay an occasional visit to a downtown furniture store owner and pass him an envelope full of cash.

That was his first objective. The second was an account book with a record of where the money had come from. According to Vallina it could be anything from a little five-by-five-inch notebook to three encyclopedia-sized volumes. And, while he had hopes of finding out something about Costa's associates, the account book seemed like a hopeless proposition. The book had probably disappeared from Costa's house on the day of his son's murder. And it had probably been the book, and not the son, which the murderers had been after.

Whatever the chances, he was determined to give it his best shot. Hector talked with three store managers, seven salesmen, one errand boy, three chauffeurs, and came up with his hands empty. Ever the positive thinker, Hector told himself that now he knew more than he had before about the furniture business, and he abandoned the city center.

"I got this idea in the metro. And it's like getting kissed by a sixteen-year-old, it's got me all fired up. I just hope you can help me with it, Red, because I don't know where else to turn."

Anita watched him, cheerful. El Horrores had set a vase of flowers on the night table. El Angel had found a guitar somewhere and was plucking out a few chords, murmuring boleros in a low, hoarse voice. Hector asked the two wrestlers to leave them alone for a minute and then started in with his disjointed account.

"I figure that what we're looking for isn't just some casual or business relationship. No one lets go of millions and millions just like that, no matter how much he trusts the other person, and without receipts or anything. The connection's got to be something more solid than a simple friendship. Except for maybe some kind of lifelong friendship, something really tight, not just your occasional drinking buddy. It had to be family. A godfather to one of his kids, a brother, something like that . . . Who were your father-in-law's closest relatives?"

"He didn't have any brothers or sisters. And I never met any cousins either. His wife died years ago. And friends, what you and I would call friends, no one I can remember. But the truth is that I'm not really the one to ask. I never liked the old man, I didn't like to go to his house. Luis and I almost never went there. Now and then for a birthday party, a Christmas dinner. But almost never."

"Who else came to Christmas dinner?"

"No one. Luis's brothers, the maid, me, the old man. That's all."

"What about presents? Think, Anita, did anybody send presents?"

"Sure, I mean there was always a bunch of big gift baskets and stuff, probably from clients, people he knew from business, that sort of thing. There wasn't anything personal that I can remember."

"Dammit, there's got to be an opening somewhere."

"What have you found out, Hector?" asked Anita.

"Not much. I know that starting in August of '76 he began acting as the under-the-table banker for someone or some group of someones. And apparently there's two different groups who're after the money now, The Rat's people and someone else. At least that's how The Rat tells it."

"You talked to him?"

"I talked to him. He says you should take your five million and get out, says to leave the rest to him, that the money doesn't belong to you."

"And what about Luis?"

"That's what I asked him. He said that the dead are dead."

"Couldn't we go to the police, to the newspapers? Make some noise?"

"I don't see how it would get us anywhere to go to the cops. El Negro Guzmán did a survey for France Press a while back, and it turned out that the police are behind something like seventy-six percent of the serious crime in Mexico City. The Rat is connected with a commander from the *judiciales*, a man named Saavedra. And who knows how many others. The men who raped you and beat you up could have been cops, who knows? As far as the newspapers are concerned, with the little we've got, I don't think they'd go for it, and they probably wouldn't even dare to print it anyway."

"So there's nothing you can do in Mexico?" asked Anita. It wasn't a bad question. Hector thought about it before answering.

"I can keep up the pressure, keep on pushing."

"Do you want to?"

"Well, I guess that even if you were to leave the country and drop the whole thing, I'd still stay on the case," said the detective. "Out of stubbornness. You don't play to win anymore, you just play to survive and to keep on fucking with the other guy."

Anita leaned back against her two pillows and sighed. The scar on her chin softened a little.

"How do you like the company?"

"They're wonderful, real sweethearts. You'd never guess it from looking at them, would you?"

"They're a couple of super guys. And honest, too. They never won a fight that wasn't rigged their way from the get-go. If pro wrestling was a serious sport they would have been two great wrestlers."

"I feel like a kid again with them around. They keep offering to bring me coffee, or to fix my pillow, or adjust the TV. And they're incredibly modest and polite. At night they take turns in the bathroom, and put on these cute little purple and green pajamas that are a couple of sizes too small. Like flood pants. Their feet hang over the end of the bed. They're real characters. And the doctors get all freaked out, they're afraid to even raise their voices."

"When are they going to let you out of here?"

"They said that I can go tomorrow. But that I have to stay in bed for another week still. Have you seen Elisa? She was here yesterday asking about you. She told me to tell you that if you don't call her she's going to punch out your good eye."

"I'll call her today, don't worry," said Hector and, lighting a cigarette, he waved good-bye. "See you later, Red."

"See you later, Detective."

He was standing in front of the hospital's main entrance when El Horrores ran up, out of breath.

"Hey, Belas, she says that if the name you said was Saavedra . . ."

"Saavedra, yeah."

"Then she says for you to get your ass back up there."

Anita was standing in a bathrobe by the bed when Hector and El Horrores came in the room.

"I'm sorry, Hector, it won't happen again. It's just that I can't think straight anymore, I'm not myself. Luis is . . . Luis's full last name was Costa Saavedra. Saavedra is his mom's name. His mom had a brother. I never met him, he never came around the house, or who knows, but I never met him. I remembered just now because of the name. Sorry I'm such an idiot."

He had lunch with Elisa in a Chinese restaurant on the corner of Insurgentes and Hamburgo. He had her bring him the keys to the Costas' house in Polanco, and she balled him out for not having called her sooner, then wheedled a shortened version of the last few days out of him. Hector, who was a poor enough storyteller to begin with, kept shifting his thoughts back and forth between what he hoped to find in the house in Polanco, the story so far, and his plate of beef strips in abalone sauce.

"So how did your writer friend feel after all that?"

"He was fine. I left him safe and sound in his apartment."

"I've read two of his books. One was a mystery novel,

and the other one was a book about this strike of women workers at a garment factory in Monterrey."

"Any good?"

"They were all right. I mean I don't think he'll win the Nobel Prize or anything, but I liked them," said Elisa with a smile. Did he owe her anything? She'd gotten him into this. She'd taken him away from the beach and the palm trees and brought him back to the city. Should he thank her?

"How do you think Anita's doing? You know her better than I do," said Hector, to break the thread of his thoughts.

"She's coming around. Those two guys you left her with are something else."

"They're buddies of mine. They're quite a pair."

"Are they for real or do they just look the part?"

"You mean do they hit for real or is it just for show?"

"Uh-huh."

"Let's just say that no one'd better try and get too close to Anita. One time El Horrores was horsing around and he gave me a backhand that broke one of my ribs."

"I made a point of being polite to them. They command respect."

"Why don't you ask them for their autographs next time you see them? They'd be thrilled. You could start a collection. I get the feeling that El Horrores and El Angel are enjoying themselves, apart from what I'm paying them. When I left them just now El Angel made sure to tell me that Anita was doing fine and not to worry about a thing. Anita can bring out the paternal instinct even in a professional wrestler."

"Yeah, in everybody except the ones who raped her and nearly killed her."

He got down from the bus in front of the Hospital Español and bought the afternoon edition of *Ultimas Noticias*. He glanced at the headlines: new offshore oil field discovered in the Gulf of Mexico; strike broken at the government-run pawn shops. He stuck the paper in his pocket, then walked a couple of blocks through the side streets of Polanco, along Lamartine. It was threatening to rain again. The house he was looking for was wedged between two buildings. It was a big place with a tiny front yard, a driveway, and an old rusted swing set in the back, left over from the three brothers' childhood, fifteen or twenty years ago. He tried the keys and got the right one on the first try. He wandered through the rooms looking for the scene of the murder. It wasn't hard to find. The rug was stained dark. After that he looked for the old man's bedroom. It was the third room he came to, after a room with *Playboy* pinups on the walls, and a bathroom with a sunken tub. So it had to be this one, with the bed with little ornate wooden feet that must have come straight from the Costa salesroom. He stopped in front of an old bureau and dug into the drawers until he found a wooden box full of old papers and photographs. He dumped the box out on top of the bed and looked through the pictures one by one until he found what he was looking for. A series of pictures from a wedding in the 1950s. The bride all in white, the furniture man in pearl gray. And standing to the couple's right, a young man of about twenty with slicked-back hair and a brand new suit. That would have to be him, either that or another one who showed up several times, in his late twenties, an arid, unfriendly face; or the smiling man with glasses who appeared in almost all of the pictures, hugging the bride and slapping the groom on the back. He put the pictures in his pocket and went out into the street. It was raining. The sidewalks were empty, Polanco had been taken over by automobiles.

On the bus on the way back he took out the newspaper again. And there, on page three, was a picture of The Rat, his head on his desk. The headline read: ARTURO MELGAR MURDERED IN HIS OFFICE. The article gave a brief summary of The Rat's public biography and went on to say that the woman who did the cleaning in the offices of National Consulting Services had found him early in the morning with a bullet in his forehead, fired at point-blank range. How had the killer gotten through The Rat's strange security system, with its up and down staircases? They'd gotten to him only a few hours after his meeting with Hector. Poor little Rat. He'd thought the system belonged to him and then the system had come and splattered his brains against the wall. So Mr. Z and his people existed after all. What was it The Rat had said? "The dead? Which ones, brother?" Well now he was one of them.

"Take a look at these pictures and tell me if you recognize anyone," said Hector as soon as the door opened.

"Hell, how old are these pictures, fifteen, twenty years?" said the writer.

"Twenty-five," said the detective.

"Lemme see, Papi," said his daughter.

"Here, take a look, Flor, but be careful, they belong to my friend the detective."

"Is he a cop?"

"No, more like a kind of democratic detective."

"Like on TV?"

"Sure, on Albanian TV, maybe. Bring us a couple of Cokes, Flor, will you. . . . This one here, this one, put another twenty, twenty-five years on him and that's Saavedra. Hell, I hardly recognize him. He couldn't be more than eighteen or twenty here, just a kid, and now he's forty-five, going bald, with a double chin, slack-jawed. Take a look for yourself," said the writer, and he pulled several magazines off a bookshelf, shuffled through them until he found a *Por Esto* with Saavedra's picture in color on the cover.

Hector compared the pictures. It was the same man. The same and different, battered by the years, a lot worse.

"Who're the rest of the people in these pictures, detective?"

"These are the wedding pictures of old man Costa and Miss Saavedra, twenty-five years ago."

"Well, whaddaya know."

The writer put on his glasses, sat down in front of his typewriter, and started to beat furiously on the keys.

"Sorry, but you caught me in the middle of something."

Hector watched the little girl come back into the room,

precariously balancing a bottle of Coke and three glasses, including a big red plastic one.

"Careful," said Hector.

"Don't worry. I've got her trained," said the girl's father.

"I'm trained," she said, staring up at the democratic detective from Albanian television.

"I've got more news," said Hector, holding out the damp copy of *Ultimas Noticias*. "Can I use your bathroom?"

"Show him, Flor. Don't let him get lost."

Hector followed, the girl dancing down the hallway.

"I'm going to be an Olympic gymnast," she said, opening the bathroom door.

"Me, too, but not until next year. This year they didn't let in any one-eyed gymnasts," Hector told her. He took a towel and dried his rain-soaked head and neck.

When Hector returned, the writer was closing the newspaper. He got up and walked over to a low table between two armchairs and poured out three Cokes.

"I was thinking about packing up and going off to Australia to write my novel. Now what do I do? Do I relax or do I start to worry for real?"

"I don't know. I suppose you could still go off to Australia to write. The Rat wasn't the one who made the decisions, or at least not the big ones. They came down to him from above. And, anyway, if you're going to go after a *judicial* commander, you already know what you're up against there."

"Who killed him?"

"Beats me. Maybe whoever's laying claim to Costa's money, rightfully or otherwise. There's a hell of a lot of money there and, if they start to fight over it, there's going to be more than one dead man."

"How about you? What've you got now? A triangle that connects the now-departed Rat with my Commander Saavedra and the Costa family. I think your novel is better than mine."

"No, what I've got is better still. I've got a connection between a guy who could get his hands on that kind of money and another guy he could trust enough to hold on to it for him. I've got what I was looking for. Why Costa? Why some lousy two-bit furniture salesman? Because they were brothers-in-law, that's why. Brothers-in-law! Give me a break."

"What's next?"

"Find out whose money it was. Where it came from. Who killed the Costa brothers."

"Why don't you ask Saavedra?"

"Why don't you ask him for me?"

"What I'm thinking is that if we don't play our cards just right, they're going to kill us both," said the writer.

They sat together by the table next to the window and watched the rain.

"This country'll kill you, Hector," said the writer, rubbing the tip of his nose for the hundredth time. "It'll kill you in a lot of different ways. It'll kill you with corruption, out of boredom, out of meanness, it'll kill you with hunger, unemployment, with cold, with bullets, it'll beat you to death. I don't mind the idea of taking a few licks at the system myself. But not like this, not like Shane, the loner, not like the wild west. Not all alone, dammit. I've spent the last thirteen years fighting the system. I was in the student movement in '68, I was active for a while in leftist politics, I worked with the unions, with factory workers, organizing, putting out magazines, pamphlets. I can't tell you how many good jobs I've left behind. I've never been interested in just making myself a bunch of money. I never worked for the PRI, I don't owe anything, or almost nothing, when I fucked up I never got anybody killed, and if I fucked somebody over it was out of ineptitude and stupidity and not because I'd sold out or was an asshole, no one ever paid me not to do what I believed in, I worked at a lot of stupid jobs but I always did things the best that I knew how. I don't want to die like this. Probably I don't want to die at all. Probably when it comes right down to it, I'll break like any other poor son of a bitch. I don't want to give in like some chump, Hector, but I'm not ready to go to war all by myself. Who am I supposed to be, Jane Fonda or something? You can't win this kind of a war, you can't even fight it. The hotshot writer and his faithful typewriter against the *judicial* commander and a thousand asshole gangsters with guns, rifles, machine guns, artillery, and bazookas. What's the deal? If the guy from the cleaners here on the corner comes to me, and says that his kid got fired from some job and they won't pay him his severance pay like the law says, then maybe I can lend a hand, and if I can write the truth and find someone to print it, then okay. But this . . .?"

They watched the rain and downed their Cokes like a pair of diabetics in a suicide pact.

"Listen, Paco, dammit," said Hector, crushing out his last Delicado in the metal ashtray. "Me detective, me big shit. Me, all I can say is that I don't know how to write my own novels, so I stick my nose into other people's. Me, all alone against the system. I've spent five years working on my style, understand? Because I'm a lousy shot. I couldn't hit an elephant at ten yards with a .38. I've got one good eye, my leg gimps up on me when it rains, yesterday I realized that my hair's going gray. I'm lonelier than a dog walking in the street and, if it wasn't for my brother and sister, I wouldn't have anybody to cry for. What's it matter? I never cry anyway. I hate it as much as you do: I can't tell you how pissed off I get watching them carve up this country, turning everything into a pile of shit. I'm as Mexican as the next guy. That's probably why all I believe in anymore is to keep on keeping on, and in fucking with them before they fuck with me. I missed '68 altogether and when I finally figured out what was going on, the tanks were already rolling into the university. I didn't read Ché until I was thirty, and then only because I was locked inside a house where there was nothing else to read. I studied engineering so that I could build bridges, cathedrals, sewers, stadiums, and I ended up as just another asshole working for General Electric. So what're you saying to me? I'm a detective because I like people."

"Turn down the TV, Flor," shouted the writer, and then asked, "Don't you want some lemon in your Coke? It tastes even better that way."

IX

THE STORY OF COMMANDER JACINTO SAAVEDRA AS ONLY HE KNEW IT

"I don't believe in the evil nature of man; I believe that his aberrations are due to a lack of imagination and a laziness of the heart."

—Ernst Toller

"A son of a bitch is a son of a bitch, and don't you forget it."

—Carlos López

When Jacinto Saavedra was twenty-two years old he sold used cars, combed his hair back with Polainds brilliantine, wore a suit to work and after hours, and took a liking to the whores in Guadalajara. That's how he ended up agreeing to front stolen cars behind his boss's back for two *judiciales* from Jalisco. He fixed them up with plates from wrecked cars which he then sold for scrap. He worked the switch, paid off his friends, and there were always five or ten thousand pesos left over at the end of every month to burn up in Tequila City.

It's not a very complicated story. One day he went along with his friends to go beat up a guy who owed another guy some money. And he liked it. He liked seeing the guy, all bloody and drooling on the ground, asking them to forgive him, to leave him alone. The only bad part about that first time were the bloodstains on his suit that not even the dry cleaners could get out. Gradually he took on more and more jobs and Jacinto Saavedra made a rep for himself as a sharp young man with balls of steel who hit good and hard for a reasonable fee. One time two *judiciales* took him up to Durango to look for three men who'd kidnapped a local cattle rancher. When they got there the rancher was already dead, and the kidnappers offered to split the ransom with them. But Saavedra and his friends decided that half wasn't good enough. Saavedra had a shotgun. He pointed it at the balls of one of the kidnappers and pulled the trigger. It was six hours before the guy bled to death. After that there was no way back, although Saavedra wouldn't have been able to see it if it had been staring him in the eyes. He worked as a bodyguard for a governor, made some money, opened up a home appliance store that went broke for lack of attention, he joined the *judiciales,* bought himself a pair of racehorses for the country fair circuit, and he ran black market stereos with some buddies on the Tijuana police force. It was an interesting life, as they say. Mostly it was a way to pass the time, while he waited for his "big chance," for his "stepping stone," for a "godfather" who would take him away from this "backwater racket", the bush leagues, and land him in the big time. It was either that or an early retirement. He married a girl from a family of Spanish shopkeepers, so he'd have someone to keep house and give him a pair of sons, and he went right on patronizing the whorehouses on the outskirts of Guadalajara. He got his chance to cash in when the federal *judiciales* recruited him to hunt down urban guerrilla groups based in Guadalajara, Monterrey, and Mexico City. They put him in charge of his own unit, and he set to work torturing suspects, murdering women, children, and close and distant relatives, ripping off refrigerators from guerrilla safe houses, and requisitioning the take from guerrilla bank robberies—half of which was handed over to his superiors at press conferences full of photographers, while the other half went to his friends and superiors behind closed doors. Then one day he walked into a Mexico City apartment looking for the brothers of a student from Jalisco by the name of Ruiz, and they dropped him with a shot from an M16. He spent two months in the hospital with a punctured lung, sweating out the lonely nights scared half to death. Following his release he liberated himself from his fear by blowing off the head of Ruiz's sixteen-year-old sister. It was then that fortune smiled on him. They sent him and his unit to guard the entrance to a Guadalajara hotel as part of a cocaine sting operation. But the story was a little more involved than that. A pair of gringo drug runners had refused to pay the standard fee to the *judiciales'* top man in Michoacán, who passed the word on to his buddies in Jalisco, who worked out their own arrangement with the gringos, which would have been just fine, except that the gringos had picked up a tail of *federales* from Sinaloa who were completely outside of the deal. The Jalisco *judiciales* had settled with the gringos for the sale of a third of the coke to two Guadalajara dealers who wanted to open up operations on another gang's turf, it being this gang that was meant to take the rap, although they'd

done what they could to cover themselves through a
banker friend who was in close with the mayor, setting
the state *judiciales* up for a shootout with the local cops.
So they agreed to float half of the third on the open
market, and agreed that one of the gang members' cousins would be the only one to take the fall, along with a
waiter in the hotel restaurant who was dealing for himself
on the side, a major sin under the circumstances. All
very simple. Except for the fact that all of this wheeling
and dealing had left the operation's other participants
with a rather excessive amount of free time on their
hands, which they proceeded to drink away in a whorehouse three blocks from the hotel that had been desig-
nated as the scene of the action. The result was that,
when things finally got under way, the shots started coming from all directions, and only Saavedra's unit knew
what it was doing, if not what was happening. In the
end, the right cops fired their assault weapons into the
wrong room, and arrested the cousin who wasn't with
the coke that wasn't, and Saavedra suddenly found himself alone in the middle of the night with three kilos of
coke and no one the wiser. It wasn't long before he
discovered that the coke had the power to open doors
and windows. That and his already impressive resumé
brought him to Mexico City, closely associated with the
new chief of the federal *judiciales* at the start of a new
administration. In the catalog of calamities that the ex-
used car salesman had compiled throughout his career,
the rules of the game were deliciously clear: Be servile
with those above you and an asshole with those below;
don't stick your nose in until you know whose ass it is;
make a lot of friends and a lot of acquaintances; hit them

when they're looking the other way; hit hard and do it twice; always be on the alert; sell out your best friend; talk like you know what's going on; don't fuck up, and when you do, rearrange the scenery enough so that they'll think it must have been somewhere else; be as smart as the smartest, but don't show off; keep your pants buttoned up around other men's wives; share your profits; don't worry what you've got to step on to survive— balls, skulls, hands, blood. By 1977 he'd finally arrived, and he decided he wanted to stay on top. It was time to embark upon a venture all his own, where he'd have to share less of what came in. After all, in the business of the Colombian traffickers he was only going to end up with a quarter share, since half of everything had to go up the ladder and then half of the other half had to trickle down. That's where Reyes and the bank jobs came in: he could hold on to everything for himself. Once he figured out how it worked, he had a mauve carpet laid in his office, he attended a course in law enforcement in Indianapolis, and he bought himself a fine selection of Italian neckties.

"My heart sank."

—*John Reed*

There were the gravediggers, Hector, and an old man in a wheelchair with a black umbrella. The whole thing took all of ten minutes. The Rat in his gray metal coffin surrounded by damp earth. Hector wheeled the old man back to the cemetery gate. He turned out to be The Rat's uncle, the only living relative, a solitary old man whose nephew had sent him money every month.

That was all. Belascoarán hadn't expected any more. No sense of hatred, nothing, just the simple routine. The Rat had passed on the same way he'd come in. If what the Buddhists said was true, he'd come back again to live the same way, and they'd shoot him through the head again, writing his name in blood on the wall behind his desk.

Hector wasn't interested in risking a return visit to the office in San Miguel Chapultepec where they'd taken him two days before, or in hunting up the obsequious driver and his bodyguard buddy. Overhead the sky spat out a fine misty rain. A sure sign that the deluge wasn't merely some bullshit prediction of Aztec sorcerers, but rather Mexico City's just and true destiny.

"Well, is she or isn't she?"

"Don Gaspar comes home every night, goes straight to bed, and sleeps like a log until about five or six in the morning, when he wakes up and then, yeah, he wants it. Hell, if I had to put up with that, I'd go looking for it somewhere else, too."

"How'd you find all this out?" Hector asked the baggy-eyed upholsterer.

"Oh, you know, just kind of investigating. Detective work, like they say."

"What about the fancy underwear?"

"Great stuff, chief. She's got these little lilac-colored panties with frilly garters and a bra with these little holes in it where her nipples stick through. . . ."

"More detective work, I assume? Or . . . let's see . . . you checked the clothesline, right?"

"That's it . . . the clothesline."

"The way I see it, there's a couple of things we can do. Either we give Don Gaspar his money back, or we make up a little white lie, or we find him a good lawyer and a bodyguard for the missus. . . . You're not married, are you?"

"Thank God."

"Well maybe this is your chance."

The upholsterer made a quick move for the door, but Hector shouted after him, "Hold on a minute! I want that money back. Not only do you take a roll in the hay with the old lady, but you think you can go ahead and keep the money too."

"Look, I did what I said I'd do. I went and figured out if she was whoring around or not."

"And?"

"She's not. She doesn't take any money for it."

"You've got a point there."

The telephone rang and Carlos Vargas took the opportunity to make his escape.

"Belascoarán."

"Vallina here. I did what you wanted. I found you a way to block it off and a way to unblock it if you want. But I need the court papers and some money to persuade a judge. I don't like it too much, Hector. Once this thing goes into motion there isn't anyone who's going to be able to get their hands on that money for the next fifty years. My phone here's already started to ring off the hook. I just tell everyone who wants to know that I'm working for UNICEF and that shuts them up pretty good. This is ugly money, Hector. It smells bad."

"Then let's go through with it. You're pretty good at this stuff, Vallina. You'd better watch out or somebody's going to think that it's your job."

"Yeah, I'm good at it; the problem is I got bad luck.

Yesterday these gringo hotshots took me out to dinner
to offer me a job with one of these multinationals here.
So what do I do? I get so drunk halfway through the
thing that I end up puking all over the boss's wife. It's
some Aztec curse."

Hector hung up. After leaving the cemetery he'd spent
the rest of the morning in the library going through the
newspaper stacks, trying to draw a connection between
the deposits in Costa's private banking operation, the
erratic movements of fresh cash, and some kind of reg-
ular source, and he'd come away with a drawerful of
notes that fit together like a German jigsaw puzzle, one
of those perfect Ravensburger ones. It made him feel
like a real detective, just like the upholsterer had said.
In a city where "what's the difference" was the all too
common answer in the face of the absolute pointlessness
of trying to do something right; a city dominated by the
primacy of appearances over actions, where "I don't give
a damn" was the everyday answer to corruption and
exploitation, doing something well was enormously grat-
ifying. Either that, or he'd quit believing in his own good
luck.

Wearing his most wrinkled jacket and his best smile,
Hector met Anita at the hospital entrance, watched over
by El Angel and El Horrores.

"She's all yours, boss. Whaddaya want us to do now?
We still got five full days paid in advance," asked El
Angel.

"Why don't you go on home, get some rest and a
change of clothes, say hi to your wives, check your kids'

grades, read the last issue of *Batallas en el Ring,* and we'll see each other tonight at my place.

"And as for you, Red, if you can find somewhere to stow that suitcase, I'll make good on that dance I promised you," said the detective. There was a spark in Anita's eyes.

"I still can't believe you really know how to dance. I don't know why, but somehow I remember that you never knew how. And seeing how you walk, I'm pretty sure you never learned."

"And how do you know how I walk?"

"Because I've watched you walk across this street from my window."

Anita was dressed in green, the redhead's uniform, and the marks left from her beating were almost gone. At least on the outside.

"Where am I going to stay?"

"For now, at my place. We need to have a long talk and figure out what we're going to do: plan A, plan B, or nothing at all. You're the boss, you know, I just work here."

"Yeah, but you don't get paid, so that means I can't tell you what to do."

"Would you feel better if you were paying me?"

"Yes."

"Fine by me."

"How's a million pesos sound?"

"You're crazy, Red."

"A million when it's over, plus expenses."

"All right. But tonight's dinner and dance are on me."

"I get dinner, too?"

"Yep. I think I'll splurge and take you out to the

taquería around the corner from my apartment. After we dance, that is."

"You're serious about this dance thing, aren't you?"

"You bet. I may be a total disaster but I keep my promises."

"And I suppose it doesn't matter if my leg still hurts and I've got a couple of broken ribs and that if we dance cheek to cheek I'll probably end up with a dislocated jaw again?"

"What of it? I've only got one eye, I've got a bum leg, and they'll never let me on the Olympic gymnastics team."

"What's that got to do with it?"

"Nothing. I just remembered this little half-Filipino girl I know."

Hector picked up the suitcase with one hand and held out his other hand to Anita, who took it with an inquisitive look. In the best tradition of late sixties' romanticism, a redheaded girl in a green dress and a detective with a suitcase crossed the Parque España hand in hand on an afternoon threatening rain. The park was quiet and peaceful. Only they were aware of how they artfully dodged kamikaze kids on bikes; repressed rapists disguised as ice cream vendors; a man pushing a little wooden bus full of children around the park, who, if he'd been born in Las Vegas, would have grown up to be a professional dealer; a housewife returning from Mass, who, if Herminio had had the balls back in 1956, would have been Queen of the Whores in Tamaulipas today; two teenagers who were, without a doubt, the local dope and bubble gum pushers; a street cop from León, Guanajuato, who'd beaten his mother to death with a

SOME CLOUDS · **129**

stone mortar; two city bureaucrats who took bribes from developers in exchange for additional water permits; and Sitting Bull's mother, condemned by poverty to sell squash seeds in the park, but who prepared love potions and strange poisoned brews at night. They fled before murderous roller skaters who, for lack of money, hadn't been able to buy the razor-sharp blades for the edges of their American-made skates. They passed a clump of peonies sheltering half a dozen African killer bees, and a self-absorbed guitarist scratching out the first notes of the anarchist hymn "Hijos del Pueblo" and dreaming of bombs in rainbow colors.

They did all this without paying too much attention, limping a little from their wounds, feeling their hands touch, leaving behind the park and its horrors, its peace and tranquility, at five-thirty in the afternoon on a day threatening rain.

Merlin the Magician had his head stuck into an old tube radio made before the Second World War, when he spotted Hector entering the building hand in hand with a redhead.

"Monsieur Belascoarán," he said very properly.

"Hey, Wiz . . . You never sent me the books you promised."

"How was I supposed to find anything in that mess of yours up there? When did you get back to town?"

The Wizard was the best landlord in Mexico City, the most affectionate with his renters, the only one who actually slid their mail underneath their apartment doors, and a neglected genius in basic electronics.

"I've been back a couple of days. I slept here last night. Who cleaned up the place, Wiz?"

"I gave the place a once-over, Hector, didn't want it to lose value on me. Nothing to worry about."

The first drops started to fall on the flower pots by the front door.

"It's going to rain again. Wiz, this is my friend Anita."

"It's a pleasure, miss. Merlin Gutiérrez at your service."

"Nice to meet you."

"It's been raining for six days straight now. Yesterday there was flooding down on the south side, on the Periferico, car wrecks and everything. This town's all screwed up. It's not supposed to rain in February. There's just no telling any more. Do you think it's ever going to stop?"

"No, Wiz. This is it. The Deluge. I hope you've got your life raft ready."

"How about an RCA Victor console with pontoons? That ought to do the trick, dammit."

Hector and Anita started up the stairs as the fat, heavy drops of rain beat the patio.

"Have you got someplace for me to hang up my X rays?" asked Anita, while Hector puttered around in the kitchen, opening up a bottle of pop and putting on water to boil for tea.

"In the bathroom, or by the bed. I always said that what this place was missing was a few good X rays and a Paul Klee poster."

"I was just asking because, well, if I'm going to be here a while . . ."

"Hey," said Hector, poking his head out the kitchen door, "you're serious about the X rays, aren't you, Red?"

"It was a metaphor, dummy."

"No, I mean, all of a sudden I remembered you were a doctor and all."

"A kidney specialist, almost. But you don't drink, so I don't think I'll do you much good."

Hector put the cup of lemon tea and the soda pop down in the middle of the floor, went over to the record player.

"What do you want to hear? I just fixed this thing yesterday."

"You probably don't have *Forever Young* by Joan Baez, do you? No, how could you?"

"Not so fast," said Hector, hunting through the stack of records. The rain slapped across the windowpane, drawing pictures. The light was fading. Anita looked around for something to sit on, then went into the bedroom, came back with a pair of pillows, and settled herself on the floor. She sipped her tea slowly. Joan Baez's warm, affectionate voice oozed from the speakers: *May God bless and keep you always, may your wishes all come true . . .*

Hector stood in the middle of the room looking at Anita.

"I can't really believe it. It's like nothing ever happened. Joan Baez and a warm house and the rain outside. I already saw this movie."

"Don't fool yourself, Red. They've probably got enough to keep them busy for the moment, with The

Rat dead and war declared. But if we keep pushing from this end, you can be sure they'll be coming after us again."

"All I want is one afternoon . . . just one. Who are they, Hector?"

"You'd better get comfortable. I'll be right back," said the detective, and he went into the kitchen to get his notebook from his jacket pocket. He came back with a bar stool and set it in the middle of the room.

"I'm going to fill in the parts I'm still not sure about. This probably isn't how it happened exactly, but the big picture's what counts. Anyway, I'll bet my left testicle that this is how it goes: In 1977, Manuel Reyes, an ex-police sergeant from the Mexico State Radio Patrol, became the country's number-one bank robber. Who knows why? Maybe he got bored of nickle-and-diming it as a state cop. Maybe he was watching too much TV. Whatever the reason, he picked up a machine gun, put his police training to good use, and started holding up banks. He never wore a mask, so it seems pretty obvious that they knew who he was from the beginning. He always worked with one or two companions and a driver. The list is endless: the Comermex in Arboledas, a Banco Nacional in Satélite, a Banco Internacional in Naucalpan, the Banco de Comercio in Ciudad Azteca . . . He started out on the outskirts of Mexico City, in Mexico State, then worked his way into town: the Banco de Comercio on Nuevo León, a Banco Nacional in the Roma, and so on. He hit so many banks so fast, it's like he was going for the world record. At least one a month. Always the same scenario, two or three armed men, with Reyes heading them up. And they didn't worry their

souls too much about having to knock off a few bank
guards along the way, or a secretary who screamed, a
few innocent bystanders. By August of '77 the newspapers were calling Reyes public enemy number one, and
Commander Saavedra, assistant chief of the *judiciales*
for Mexico City, was put in charge of the manhunt. It's
not hard to figure out what happened next. And it didn't
take long for Reyes and Saavedra to reach an under-
standing. That's where your father-in-law, Costa, comes
in. One day Commander Saavedra, Costa's dead wife's
brother, comes to visit him at the furniture store and
asks him if he can hold on to some money for him. Take
a look at this. On one side you've got a list of Reyes's
booty, and on the other you've got Costa's investments.
In December '77 Reyes holds up a bank on Toluca Avenue, kills a guard on the way in, walks away with two
and a half million pesos. On December 13 Costa buys
two boutiques in the Zona Rosa and one in Monterrey,
then deposits one hundred seventy-five thousand in a
bank account, for a total of two million three hundred
fifty thousand. Here's another one: a bank robbery on
Insurgentes, January 17, 1978, one and a half million.
On the nineteenth, Costa buys a million three hundred
thousand pesos in gold centenarios and puts them in a
safe deposit box. You've got Reyes making the hits on
the one hand, Saavedra as middle man, and on the other
hand there's Costa playing banker. There's about fifteen
coincidences like this all together, and if it doesn't work
out just right, it's probably because Costa didn't always
get the money right away, or the gang spent it on safe
houses, guns, cars, whores, whatever, or because Costa
was saving up a bunch to buy some business or some-

thing. If it wasn't for that, and maybe because we've missed a few safe deposit boxes, it'd all add up to the last cent. So, everything was going along just fine, until last December, when two things happened.

"First, Reyes was arrested during a botched holdup, when a wounded bank guard shot him in the leg and his buddies escaped without him. He's still in jail now. Then Costa died of a heart attack. After that I can only speculate. With Reyes in jail, the rest of the gang decides to take their money and get out while they can. Saavedra doesn't have access to Costa's accounts and has to put the gang off. Remember we're talking about nearly two hundred million pesos split five ways: Reyes in jail, Saavedra at police headquarters, and the rest of them on the run. Then somehow, Luis's two brothers get mixed up in the story. Who killed them? Saavedra? Reyes's gang? Obviously, they tried to get them to sign the money over. From what you told me about the older brother, maybe he thought he could deal with them, cut himself in. Whatever happened, he ended up dead, and the other brother was so flipped out he wasn't much good to anyone any more. Think about how they feel, they're desperate. Two years' worth of robberies come off without a hitch, and then their banker dies on them and they can't get to the money. That's when Luis shows up. And I really don't know what happened there, when he got killed in New York, if it was just an accident, an absurd coincidence, or if they hired someone to kill him. If that's the case, then everything points to Saavedra, because I just can't see the other ones playing gangster in New York. But it doesn't make any sense, anyway, because they needed an heir in order to be able to get at the money. Saavedra couldn't operate in the open, so he hired The Rat to put pressure on you and get at the money that way. But Reyes's gang apparently didn't feel like waiting around, so they came after you and had you sign the papers. Who knows what they thought they were going to do with them? It's easier to rob a bank than to legally get the money from an inheritance that's already changed hands three times in one month. Then they got desperate, killed The Rat . . . and that's where we are now."

Hector took a long drink from his soda pop.

"There's more. Your father-in-law had a hard time figuring out what to do with all that money, and what he did do with it is pretty confusing. Running three furniture stores is one thing, managing two hundred million pesos in assorted investments is something else. But there is a pattern. Part of the money went to Guadalajara, that's where Saavedra and your husband's mother are from. Another part went up to Monterrey and the northwest, and another part went to Puebla, where Reyes is from. You know what they say, there's no place like home. The other thing is that I've got descriptions of two of Reyes's cronies. All I've got is a nickname for one of them, they called him John Lennon, he's blond, acne all over his face, about five-ten. The other one is another ex-cop named Luis Ramos. This is him in the picture."

"That's the short one, the one who looked like Chelo."

"There it is, then. Now all that's left to do is wrap it up, tie a ribbon around it, and figure out what to do with it."

"What can you do?" Anita asked. The automatic return still didn't work on the record player, despite Hector's fix-it job, and the needle danced up and down on the last groove.

"Protect us from Reyes's friends and hope that Saavedra doesn't know we know about his connection to the story. He's the one I'm really worried about. I got Vallina to find a loophole in the will and set up a way to freeze the money. Of course, you could always just give it all away, and they wouldn't have any reason to come after you any more."

"Who would I give all that money to?"

"Beats me. Think about it a while."

"What happens if we go public with the whole thing?"

"I'm not too sure it would do us any good. There've been accusations in the papers against nearly every top police officer in Mexico City, and nothing ever happens. There just isn't that much the press can do for us. As far as going to the cops is concerned, I can just see the two of us filing charges at the public attorney's office. They'd laugh us back out onto the street."

"Makes you want to push all the furniture against the door and crawl under the bed," said the redhead.

"We could do it on top of the bed just as easy," said Hector, regretting it almost as soon as the words were out of his mouth, when he saw the surprise in Anita's eyes.

She got up without saying a word and went into the bathroom. Hector stepped over and picked up the needle, flipped the record over, and Joan Baez returned to compete with the sound of the rain on the glass.

What the fuck was he doing? Did he think he was doing himself some kind of favor? Or performing an act of redemption for Anita's sake? Because they'd killed her husband and raped her and beat her nearly to death? Or was it for real, and was there something truly magical about this little redheaded woman that made him want to love her or that made him love her already? Hector had read an Ecuadorian poet once who'd said that you could also kill "through loneliness, through fear, through fatigue." He didn't like what he'd just done. He walked toward the bathroom to apologize, and found Anita standing naked in front of the mirror. Or nearly naked, with a piece of adhesive tape still covering a spot on her left leg, and a two-inch strip of gauze wrapping itself around her torso just below her breasts.

"I was just looking at myself. I don't know if I'm ready yet," she said, two big tears rolling down her cheeks.

"Come here. I'm an idiot," said Hector, and he hugged her gently, put his cheek against her hair, and rocked her with his arms. Anita squeezed herself against him. Hector put a towel across her shoulders, decided against it, because the towel might be dirty, took it off, picked her up in his arms, and carried her to the bed where he tucked the sheet up under her chin. He started out, meaning to go and meditate on his stupidity alone in the other room, but Anita's voice caught him at the door.

"I'm not going to let you get away that easy. Come over here, silly. It was your idea."

The doorbell saved him, and he went to open up for the wrestlers, taking the opportunity to get away from the confusion inside his head. Anita let out a soft laugh that chased her tears.

He opened the door with a big smile, but a fist to the mouth was all it took to tell him that, for the second time that afternoon, he'd made a mistake.

XI

"Oftentimes the persecuted lose the ability to recognize their own faults."

—*Bertolt Brecht*

The blow sent him flying backward into the kitchen stool in the middle of the room. He went down and, spinning around, brought his hand to his gun, but the holster was empty; he'd left the gun with his jacket in the kitchen. The short, stocky one threw a kick at his ribs, and Belascoarán rolled to the side, shouting inside his head at Anita not to come out of the bedroom.

"Don't move, asshole," said the blond one with the acne tattoo.

A third man came in and shut the door. He wore a gray suit at least a size too big for him. He held a .45 automatic in his hand.

"Where is she?"

"I left her at her house."

"Look at that, the guy's real quick. He already knows what we're talking about and everything. So we don't have to waste no time. What house?"

While Hector stared down the barrel of the automatic, Blondy caught him with the promised kick to the ribs. It doubled him over like a punching bag, but he held in the pain, the shout, only grunting softly.

"What house, asshole?"

"The one in Polanco."

"Bullshit. There's nobody there. Where'd you stash her?"

The dark, short one jerked Hector up by the back of his sweater, punched him in the face, dropped him.

"Shit, man, you poked his eye out."

Shorty grabbed Hector's face in one hand. He laughed.

"It isn't real. It's all scarred over. Must be a glass eye."

"Give it back to him," said the man by the door. "So he can see us better."

"What'd The Rat tell you about us?" Shorty asked, handing Hector his glass eye, not wanting to hold on to it for very long. Hector threw it to one side.

"Who are you?" asked the detective to gain time.

Blondy picked up the kitchen stool, set it on its legs, sat down, and kicked Hector's foot softly with the toe of his boot.

"What'd The Rat tell you? Did he say the money wasn't ours, did he tell you to give it to him?"

Hector yanked out a tuft of carpet. Without knowing where it came from, he held it in his clenched fist. If Anita could get from the bedroom into the kitchen where his gun was . . . but he'd have to distract them. He got up and stumbled toward the side of the room with the record player. Shorty stopped him.

"There's just two things. Where is she? And what'd The Rat tell you? That's all we want to know. That isn't too complicated, is it?"

He hit Hector twice, jackhammer style, in the stomach. Hector felt the air leave his lungs. He dropped to the floor, gasping for breath. Anita would never make it to the kitchen.

"Let's burn the soles of his feet, like Cuauhtémoc," laughed Blondy.

Hector pulled in air, let out something between a shout and a groan, gasped, crawled toward the stool. Shorty grabbed him by the foot; the shoe came off in his hand.

"The stupid son of a bitch has a hole in his sock." He laughed.

Hector shot out his other foot and caught the leg of the stool. Blondy saw what was coming, stood halfway up, went over backward with the stool, knocking his head against the record player. Blood spilled from Blondy's split lip, but Hector barely had time to appreciate it, because Shorty, still holding on to his other foot, drove a fierce kick into his thigh.

"Let's get down to business, dammit," said the man with the gray suit and the gun, just as the door started to open behind him. He turned around, but not quickly enough, because a hand appeared in the opening. The hand held a clothes iron, which slammed down on the man's wrist. He yelped and dropped the gun.

The Wiz materialized behind the iron. In his other hand he held a ring of keys. Shorty brought his hand to the gun in his belt, but he had to let go of Hector's foot, and the detective sent him with a kick toward the open door, and into the arms of El Angel, who had followed the landlord into the room.

Hector turned to see Blondy coming at him with a knife. An enormous hand settled softly on the detective's shoulder and moved him to the side. El Horrores advanced on Blondy, who threw himself into reverse, drawing circles in the air with the knife. El Horrores gave him a flying kick, one foot crushing the knife arm, the other foot clipping Blondy on the chin. The apocryphal John Lennon crashed backward. Behind him, Hector heard the crack of Shorty's neck snapping under El Angel's full Nelson. The Wiz stood warily by the door, the iron in one hand, the automatic in the other, the gray-suited man unconscious at his feet.

"You want me to get rid of him, Hector?" asked El Horrores, holding Blondy in the air and stepping toward the window.

"Get rid of him."

Blondy kicked and sobbed uselessly as the wrestler held him by the belt and the back of the shirt.

"Open it for me, willya, Hector? This one's too soft to break through on his own."

Hector opened the window. His mouth tasted of blood.

"I didn't see anything," said the Wiz from his post at the doorway.

Blondy screamed hysterically through the open window. Hector looked at him without hearing.

"Leave him on the floor."

El Horrores threw the blond man against the wall like an old doll. Wall and body met with a dry thud, knocking a photograph of Hector's father's boat off its hook. The

detective took two steps and let himself fall into the
wrestler's arms. Then he stumbled past him into the hall
that led to the bedroom. Anita held the pillow in her
mouth to keep from screaming, her eyes bulging with
terror. Hector ran his hand softly along her naked shoulder and she started to shout.

"I wanted to help you but I couldn't! I swear, Hector,
I couldn't! I couldn't do it! I couldn't move!"

"It's all over now, Anita. It's time to get dressed."

When he heard the first sirens, Hector picked up the
phone and called Marciano Torres at *Uno más uno*.
Torres arrived with a photographer five minutes after the
two uniformed cops entered the apartment with their
guns drawn. Anita had been quickly relocated to the
Wiz's apartment, and the three bank robbers occupied
various positions on the floor. Blondy was crumbled
against the wall, in shock, where El Horrores had thrown
him. Shorty was dead, his neck broken. The one in the
gray suit sprawled in a corner moaning, holding on to
his broken wrist. The two cops called in a backup squad
car, and the backup cops called in some more. The puls-
ing red and blue lights filled the street with party colors.
Torres's photographer moved around the room, his flash
popping. Hector washed his face and went into the bedroom to look for his eye patch. He was limping badly.

"Get these two out of here and take the dead one
down to the ambulance," ordered a police sergeant,
who'd taken control, directing the search of the room,
collecting the guns and the knife from the floor. Hector
had explained to him how the men were members of the

Reyes gang, how they'd come to kill him, and how, purely by coincidence . . . The sergeant left him in mid-sentence and went out to the street. He came back ten minutes later. Hector stood in the kitchen, drinking a soda pop with the wrestlers, Torres, and the photographer.

"Commander Saavedra wants to talk to you," he said.

"Don't let me out of your sight, brother," Hector told the reporter. "I'll fill you in on the details later."

He sat in the back of the squad car, siren wailing, followed by the reporter's car, and another squad car with the two surviving bank robbers. The city, awash with rain, seemed more unreal than ever.

Saavedra sat behind a metal desk. He was a nervous man, with a tic shuddering along the left side of his mouth. He was light-skinned, balding on top but with his hair longish down the sides, cold blue eyes, slightly overweight for his short five-foot-four-inch frame. He wore a deep red suit and a white shirt. When he turned, his open jacket revealed a glimpse of the gun at his hip.

"I want to congratulate you," he said, holding out a hand adorned with two gaudy rings. Hector held back, holding his right arm with his left hand.

"Sorry, I must have broken it in the fight," he said, staring at Saavedra.

"You should have said something to the sergeant. You could have had it taken care of before you came. There wasn't any hurry. I only wanted to . . ."

The detective dropped into a swivel chair, with Torres, the photographer, and the two wrestlers by his side. A few plainclothesmen stood around and watched. Two more photographers, probably from the judicial police PR office, flashed away at a smiling Commander Saavedra and an exhausted detective slumped in a swivel chair.

"We've been tracking these men down for months, the last members of Reyes's gang of bank robbers," announced the commander, as if he were at a press conference. "And now this stroke of luck has brought them into custody. In the name of the department and the officers assigned to this case, I want to publicly thank these citizens and acknowledge their civic valor."

Torres pretended to take notes, the photographers clicked and flashed.

"My men are waiting to take your statements," said Saavedra. He eyed the detective coldly and left the room.

"What the hell's going on around here?" Torres asked Belascoarán.

"He's up to his ears in shit, that's what."

"Who, Saavedra?"

"Who else?"

XII

"Man who eats his heart poisons himself."

—*Sabu*

It was four in the morning when Hector woke Elisa up at their parents' old house in Coyoacán. It wasn't Elisa he'd come to see, but the old .22 automatic that their father had left among the papers and books in the library when he died. It was the second time he'd made the sentimental journey back for the pistol. Elisa, in a white nightgown that brushed the floor, her hair standing out strangely around her head, followed him in silence to the library, which was dominated by an oil portrait of their father dressed in the uniform of the Spanish merchant marine.

Hector picked up the leather box, took out the gun,

weighed it in his hand, then dropped into an armchair. He leaned back, winced, grunted sharply.

"What's wrong?"

"A couple of hours ago someone kicked me in the leg, punched me in the stomach, knocked out my glass eye, slapped me in the face, kicked in my ribs, and then this son of a bitch tried to shake my hand. Is that enough?" he said, almost immediately regretting having said so much.

"I'm sorry, Hector. I didn't realize what it meant to get you involved in this."

"It's okay. You're not the one I've got to settle with. It's . . ." and he sat thinking about who, about what. With Saavedra, of course. He kept seeing the tic twisting at the corner of Saavedra's mouth, over and over. The image was clear, almost cinematographic. But Saavedra wasn't everything. He had a score to settle with the violence, the fear, Anita's terror.

"Can I get you something?" asked Elisa at his side, uncertain.

"Two aspirins and a glass of milk, isn't that what Mama always used to say?"

The library was nearly dark. Elisa had turned out the ceiling light, leaving only the two softly illuminated lamps with their wide shades that the old man had kept on his desk. That's how it had always been. Elisa remembered too.

"He's going to kill me. That son of a motherfucking bitch is going to kill me."

"Who, Hector? What the hell did I get you into?" Elisa brought a hand to her head and nervously tried to smooth out her hair.

"Forget it, Elisa. I can do without the waterworks." The words sounded good there, in that room. It was something their father used to say. "If you hadn't come for me I'd probably have been run over by a bicycle on the beach and died anyway."

"Ten days, that's all it's been. Ten days," Elisa said in a tight voice.

"Just leave me alone, Elisa. Let me be here for a while. I'm beat. I need to recharge. When I looked at Saavedra, I saw my death in his eyes."

"Where's Anita?"

"Anita's all right. She's with the Wiz, in his apartment, with the wrestlers. She's not the one they want, anyway. They want me now. I could see it in the motherfucker's eyes."

Elisa looked her brother over carefully. He was pale, with pain showing in his dull eyes, his feverish lips. She stood next to the leather armchair, not knowing what to do. As if watching over the dead.

"Go back to sleep, Elisa, please. I've got to go this one alone. It's inside me. I've got to figure out how to bust the whole thing open, how to break it all into so many pieces that there's no way they could put it back together again. It can't be that hard. He can't sleep now, either. He's rolling around in his bed, or sitting up in his office, thinking how everything's about to come crashing down on top of him. How, if things start to break, his bosses'll cut him loose, or, what's worse, take it one step further, bust his head in with a stapler or something. They don't give a shit about your crimes, it's being stupid enough to get caught that they can't stand for. That's the rules they play by and he's breaking the rules. So

Commander Saavedra's not getting any sleep either,'' said Hector, a smile spreading across his face. A smile that scared Elisa.

"Can I get you something, Hector? You want something?"

"How about a Coke with lime," said Hector, his smile warmer now.

Hector laughed when he saw the searching way that his brother Carlos was looking at him. The two of them must have been talking about him. He stretched his legs and pulled off the plaid blanket Elisa had covered him with during the night. In the end it had been Hector who slept, and not Elisa. From the bags under her eyes, she must have spent the whole night watching over him, blaming herself. *Shit, I never should have come here. It's not Elisa's fault,* thought the detective. And then, as if to defend himself from the load that Carlos was about to dump on him, he yawned.

"You've got too much of a bourgeois attitude toward this whole thing, Hector," Carlos said seriously, after hearing his brother's story. "The violence comes straight from the system, when are you going to figure that out?"

Hector was back in form now. He'd had a glass of orange juice and ham and eggs on the patio with his brother and sister, he'd called the Wiz to check on Anita, and he could feel the life flowing through his veins again.

"The thing that really gets me is that the guy wanted to shake my hand, and I almost did it, I really almost did it," he said. "That's what pisses me off the most."

"You're looking at it all wrong, Hector. You make it sound like the city's falling apart, like all of a sudden the gangsters are running the show. It's true, but it didn't start yesterday. Maybe you're right, maybe they've got more room to move in than usual. There are more hired thugs going around than ever before, that's for sure. Every two-bit bureaucrat's got forty bodyguards waiting to run you off the road so their boss can get to work on time. Or like when they shut off four square blocks downtown so that the president's sister can go out for *churros* and chocolate for breakfast. They get drunk and start horsing around and blow someone's cousin away by accident. They run some guy off the Periferico for not getting out of the way fast enough. But that's the way it is. The cops in this town are as big a cesspool as they are because there's big money involved. You know what happens to the lowly motorcycle cop who puts the bite on you for three hundred pesos because you ran a stoplight? At the end of the day he has to kick back fifteen hundred or two grand to his sergeant for letting him work the good intersections, and if he doesn't, he'll be out sweeping streets or directing traffic, left to eat shit. The guy has to pay for the maintenance on his own bike, because if he takes it to the shop at the station they'll steal everything down to the spark plugs and, boom, the guy's back on the streets again, on foot. And he starts every day with eight liters of gas instead of the twelve he's allotted, because his major and his chief skimmed off the other four. He pays into a pension plan that doesn't exist, and a life insurance pool that doesn't exist either. His sergeant kicks back twenty-five grand to the district chief, who runs hot license plates on the side and takes a bite out of the phony pension fund. You know how the commanders call roll at the start of each day at district headquarters? With an envelope in their hand. Officer so-and-so reporting for duty, and there goes the money into the envelope. The district commander must take in half a million pesos every day. He's got two officers and all they do is collect money. . . . *That's* the system, not a measly three hundred peso bribe. . . . You have to take a step back to be able to see the system."

"Enough, Carlos. The last thing I need right now is a consciousness-raising session. I believe everything you say, but either I figure out some way to stop Saavedra, or pretty soon you're going to be lighting candles at my funeral."

"Try and look at it philosophically, brother," said Carlos, brushing the hair out of his face and lighting up a cigarette. "All you've got to do is find the crack in the system. Saavedra belongs to a scumbag set, they own him, and if he starts to get in the way, they'll throw him in the garbage can. All you have to do is make it so they throw him away."

"The only thing I've been able to think of isn't any good. It's the simplest way. To bring everything together and turn it over to the newspapers. Some of them would go for it. Torres said he'd get the foreign journalists on it, too, to turn up the pressure. The only problem is that the story I've got doesn't hold together. I know it's true. Torres knows it's true. Saavedra knows it's true. If the cops hadn't arrived so soon I could have found out if those assholes had Costa's account book or not. But if they did have it, it's too late now, because Saavedra'll have it stuck away safe in a desk drawer somewhere. So there's nothing I can do there. Of course, I can still take away their main reason for wanting to come after Anita and me. That is, she can shut off the money, give it all to UNICEF, like Vallina said, or to the guerrillas in Honduras."

"El Salvador. If that's what you want it won't be hard."

"El Salvador, whatever. But that still leaves me with the same problem. Whatever happens, Saavedra's going to want his revenge."

"Get on an airplane. We've still got the money Papa left us."

"Do it, Hector, take a plane. And Anita too," said Elisa, leaving off biting her fingernails for a moment. "Or if you want, we can get on my bike and I'll take you back to that beach of yours."

"Sorry, little sister. There's no going back anymore."

XIII

"Upon what dead man do I live, his bones inside my own?"

—*Roberto Fernández Retamar*

He waited while the diminutive redhead disappeared up the escalator, then roamed around the airport until he could watch the KLM jet take off. Shiny, like a toy, splitting the air with its noise. Endings are so abrupt, Hector thought, only beginnings have grace. Endings are short, unpleasant, without an overtime where you can object to the way things worked out.

He walked toward the metro station. On his back he could feel the eyes of the men following him. He didn't care enough to try and lose them. For now they only followed, keeping their distance, settling the weight of their stares on his back, eyes he wouldn't see from straight on. He walked along Bucareli, dodging the bicycle acrobatics of the newspaper vendors. At the entrance to the building on Donato Guerra, where he had his office, he saw Don Gaspar getting into the elevator, and turned on his heel.

He headed back to his apartment, following aimless detours, as if he wasn't in a hurry to get anywhere.

The glass from the photo of his father's boat still lay broken on the rug, by the fallen frame. He collected the bits of glass on a sheet of newspaper and rehung the picture on the wall. Then he threw himself onto his bed. What was he waiting for? The money was taken care of. Torres couldn't risk breaking the story without more proof to link Saavedra with the bank robbers and Costa's money. Anita was safe, thirty thousand feet up in the air. She'd given up her inheritance and no one could touch her now, except maybe the Cancer Society, to whom she'd donated the money.

So what was Saavedra waiting for?

Hector took out his gun and played with the chamber. He removed the clip and took out the bullets one by one, replaced them again. The phone rang.

"He's dead, brother. Either he got himself killed or they killed him, in an accident out on the highway to Queretaro."

"Who, Saavedra?"

"Yeah, but your writer friend was with him. They both bought it. Together. They're calling it an accident. I saw it on the TV news. They were going over a hundred when they ran into a semi. . . . That's the official story, anyway. Who knows." His brother Carlos's voice came over the telephone.

"They were together?"

"Yeah. Just the two of them in the car."

"He doesn't deserve to die with that son of a bitch," said Hector, and he hung up.

Two days later a laconic, tardy telegram appeared under Belascoarán's apartment door while he was heating up some chicken bouillon. It said: "I'VE GONE TO ASK HIM. PACO IGNACIO."

As they were leaving the cemetery, Elisa looked up at the sky and took hold of Hector's arm, stopping him. Sixteen days ago she'd looked up at the sky through palm trees, another sky.

"Look at those clouds. It's going to pour."

"Then they must be clouds of shit," said Hector, without raising his eyes.